A WITCHY LIFE FOR ME

WICKED WITCHES OF PENDLE ISLAND BOOK 10

MARA WEBB

CHAPTER 1

"There, we're…finally…done!" I said in exhaustion, clearing the last inquiry from my inbox and slamming my laptop shut. I dropped my head onto the table and let out a long sigh of relief.

"I can't believe you actually did it!" Artemis said. He was sitting atop the table licking the back of his paw. "Six hundred mysteries in one month! That's got to be a record!"

"We should celebrate!" Lizzy said. She dipped a biscuit into her tea and frowned as half broke off and sank into the milky brew. "You're on a roll, Chelsea!"

"First of all, I didn't solve six hundred mysteries," I said. "So, let's clear that up straightaway. A lot of the inquiries in my inbox were absolute junk."

I'd only recently found out I had a website where my skills as an amateur investigator were offered to the public. My familiar, Artemis, had set the site up for me without my knowledge several months ago. Artemis had—in classic Artemis fashion—advertised the website, completely forgot to tell me anything about it and only brought it up recently, leaving me with a massive backlog of potential cases to work through.

As it turned out there was a lot of junk in that inbox, so it wasn't like I'd been running around the island on turbo speed for two weeks, solving forty-two mysteries a day—yeah, I'd done the math.

During my time here on Pendle Island I'd stumbled across a number of mysteries, wound up solving them and ended up in the local newspaper as a result. Thanks to that my website—which I knew nothing about until recently—was steadily gaining requests for that entire length of time.

I was something of a local celebrity now, not that I enjoyed acknowledging that. Every time I walked down the street strangers would stare at me, generally be excited to see me, or run over to have their picture taken. It had gotten to the point now where I was considering leaving the house in a baseball cap and shades. A ten-minute trip to get bagels the other day turned into a half an hour excursion after getting cornered by a group of old women in the mall.

Of the six hundred inquiries over *half* of them were from people that didn't even live on the island. As I didn't want to do any traveling back to the mainland, I dismissed them straightaway, quickly filing through them to sort the wheat from the chaff. Most of the requests were not pressing matters, a surprising amount of people were willing to hire me to help them look for their remote, or a pair of keys. *Yeah... not interested!*

There were three of four mainland inquiries that did seem a little more pressing, so I passed the details onto my fiancé, Deacon, to forward to his police colleagues over the sea.

That left three hundred inquiries from the island itself. One hundred of those were from the same person, 'Colin Peepers' an old man who was looking for his lost cat. Colin, as it turned out, wasn't that tech savvy, and had accidentally sent the same message one hundred times: *Dear Chelsea Sponks, my name is Colin Peepers, and I'm looking for my lost cat, Beepers! My fax number is...*

Alongside this were nonsense inquiries from crazy people: *My neighbor is stealing my pickles,* or *The Irish have a secret hideout in the sewers,* or *The Egyptian artifacts in Pendle Museum are fakes!*

When I finally finished whittling down the inquiries, I found fifty that weren't written by crazy people, and of those fifty over half were from people asking me to spy on their spouse and see if they were cheating. I forwarded *those* requests to an actual PI friend of Deacon's; I didn't have any interest in being some sort of love doctor.

That left me twenty-five legitimate inquiries and even then, most of them were requests about missing pets. After these last two weeks I might as well have called myself Chelsea Sponks, Pet Detective, because I'd spent the better part of the month hunting down missing cats, dogs, hamsters, and even one chinchilla. I'd even found Beepers, Colin Peepers' cat. It turned out Beepers had two different homes and had been with Colin's next-door neighbor the entire time. It's amazing what the most basic of questions will turn up.

Among the missing animal cases there were a few petty theft cases that didn't prove too troubling either, in fact the entire lot was—all in a word—tame. There were no murders, no grand heists, no ancient cold cases, no missing person's cases.

It was almost like the island was starting to get soft on me.

"Still though, clearing through all that junk, that's something worth celebrating," Artemis commended.

"Yeah…. I guess so," I said with a note of indifference.

"You're hungry for something real, aren't you?" Lizzy asked with a knowing smile.

"There's still pressing matters at hand," I said. There were still some important things on my laundry list, things that *did* require my attention sooner than later. A mysterious cult had sprung up in Babonix, a skiing town on the northern side of the island.

In addition to that it seemed a coven of evil witches named the Brewdocks were on the return and trying to take over the island. They were supposedly based on a little isle out west of Pendle Island called Vassago Isle. I'd been putting off the visit because to be honest I was a little bit scared.

"But you're making a killing as a Pet Detective!" Artemis said. "These last two weeks have been among your most lucrative!"

"It's definitely putting bread on the table," Lizzy remarked sarcastically.

"Hey, don't get me wrong, there is an *unusual* amount of money in tracking down people's lost animals, but the work isn't exactly mentally stimulating, if you know what I mean. If I wanted to spend the rest of my life coaxing animals out of bushes, I'd work for the town's animal control."

"One of my old friends from school works for animal control!" Lizzy said excitedly. "Do you want me to pass your details on?"

"I was uh… being sarcastic, Lizzy," I said. "Still, I do *have* things to do, I've just been putting them off. The whole business with the Brewdock witches… I don't know why I'm pushing that one back."

Two weeks ago, a giant spell took over the island, transforming every inhabitant to a teenage version of themselves. A huge high school appeared at the center of town, and everyone was lost under this general amnesia, living under the fake veil of the spell, convinced we were real teenagers.

Thanks to my familiar Artemis and my brother Rudy I managed to break out of the illusion, and we tracked the spell's culprit, Alison Brewdock. The Brewdock witches were apparently an old enemy of the Sponks witch family and a few of them now lived on Vassago Isle, a small lump of rock west of Pendle Island, something I only found out about recently.

There was apparently a castle on that island, and underneath that castle lay some ancient magical power. The vampire that used to live in the castle couldn't go back because of the witches now living there and had tasked me with fixing the problem.

I guess I'd partly been putting off the trip to the isle because I *was* scared of these Brewdock witches. There was no telling what they could do. Their last attempt to take over the island had nearly worked, and they had displayed some seriously strong magic. Still, I suppose I had to confront them sooner or later—they were only going to get stronger with time.

"I should bite the bullet and just go over there," I surmised. "Still… it's probably wise to gather backup."

"I'll get my knuckle dusters!" Lizzy said. "And I can call Aunt Glenda too!"

Glenda alone was a force to be reckoned with. The three of us could probably hold our own against this group of evil witches. It's not like I was intending to go over there to fight. My first port of call was to see what they wanted, and if we could reason with them.

The only problem was that Glenda and Lizzy usually skipped the reasoning part and got straight to the ruckus. Unfortunately, they were two of the strongest witches on this island apart from myself, and nobody else could fill their shoes.

"Still that *cult* business up in Babonix is pretty pressing," I countered. "It could be worth checking that out before I make this journey over to Vassago Isle."

"Boo!" Artemis jeered. "Stop putting it off! You're only delaying the inevitable!"

"Ugh, you're right," I sighed. "I just need to put together a team, take a boat over there and see what those Brewdock witches want."

"Total control, world domination!" Artemis wailed dramatically. Lizzy and I shot him a disapproving look. "What? I'm bored. I'm trying to add a little drama to the mix. Spice things up a little bit."

"Why don't I call Glenda and we can head over there tomorrow?" Lizzy queried. "I'm pretty curious about this Vassago Isle anyway! I've lived on Pendle Island all my life and never heard anything about it!"

"How do we even get over there?" I asked. "It looks like it's thirty minutes at least by boat. I'd suggest plane, but they don't have a runway from the looks of things."

"You have a boat," Artemis reminded me. "You inherited it from Griselda, along with the house!"

I hadn't actually forgotten about the boat, but I had seen the thing in person a few months ago and I very much doubted its ability to make even a journey that small. My 'boat' was a tiny barnacle-encrusted thing, and it could just about fit me on my own, let alone three of us. "Disregarding the fact that I don't have any sailing experience—"

"Me neither," Lizzy added. "Glenda does actually, but her license is suspended. It's a long story."

I stared at my cousin for a moment. "Right... well disregarding *that*, even if I did know how to sail I sure as heck wouldn't step foot on that rusting coffin that Griselda called a boat. Have you seen that thing Artemis? It's a death trap!"

"Yeah, it's probably a decade or two past its prime," he admitted. "Still, there are water taxis you can hire to get over there. Heck, get Deacon to take you over! The police department *has* boats, and Deacon can sail!"

"Wait, he can?" I said in amazement. Somehow that had never come up before. "Still, he's with his family until the end of the week. They're still dealing with the loss of his brother."

The spell that had taken over the island recently wasn't without its causalities. Alison Brewdock, the evil witch behind the giant illusion, had killed two people to fuel the magical energy needed for her ritual. One of them was an old librarian in Pendle Island's Magical Archives, and the other was Deacon's brother.

Ever since then Deacon had been on grievance leave, and he was currently back on the mainland spending time with his family. I had only discovered recently that Deacon's family were obscenely wealthy, something that Deacon left behind when he came to the island to make a quiet life for himself.

Deacon's relationship with his family was strained, he had somehow grown up in that world and turned out relatively normal, though his mother, father, and siblings were all quite out of touch. Brian, Deacon's youngest brother that had just passed away, had grown up in a South American nunnery with Deacon when they were both young, being sent there by their parents to 'toughen them up'.

In fact, it did the opposite and both Deacon and Brian turned out to be normal people with a distaste for their affluent upbringing. Despite his estrangement with his family Deacon and Brian were close, so his brother's death had hit him hard. By all accounts it seemed the death itself had brought the family closer together. Deacon hadn't spent this much time with his family in years, and from my conversations with him on the phone it sounded like his time back at home was going well.

"There are plenty of men with boats on this island just itching for an excuse to get out on the water," Lizzy said. "I'm sure we can find someone to ferry us across. I'm up for tomorrow if you're up for it."

"Alright, I guess I can't put this off any longer. Give Glenda a call and we'll lock it in. Hey, at least I've got all those email inquiries done and dusted. I can take the rest of the day off and maybe do some gardening!" Just then my phone pinged, and from the notification on the screen I could see I had a new message in my inbox on the website. "You've gotta be kidding me! A new request already!"

"The devil makes work..." Lizzy smirked as I opened up the laptop.

"Ooh let me guess!" Artemis chirruped excitedly. "A dumb dog is stuck in a toilet!"

Lizzy joined in. "No, don't tell me! They've lost the bingo spinner at the old person's home!"

"Hah hah," I said dryly. "You know you're both *very* funny. You should have a double act on stage. Let's see what we've got here..."

I opened my inbox for the website and saw the subject line, my interest caught straightaway: *Chelsea Sponks! Old Cold Case with $100k reward!*

"Woah," I said, leaning back in my chair slightly.

"What is it?" Artemis asked. "Two dogs stuck in a toilet?!"

"An old cold case with a six-figure reward," I said, relaying the email subject to them. I was about to open the email when the door-bell chimed. I stood up, wondering what the message could possibly be about.

"Don't leave us hanging!" Lizzy groaned.

I walked out of the kitchen and opened the front door. Standing on my porch was a young woman with electric blue hair, she couldn't have been much more than five feet tall. She thrust a huge micro-phone in my face.

"Chelsea Sponks, I'm Adina Lopez, the host of Fools n' Ghouls, the internet's most in demand true crime paranormal podcast! Do you have a comment regarding rumors that you have taken up the old murder cold case involving construction giant Declan King?!"

I had to step back, blindsided by the pint-sized woman barking questions on my front porch. I put my palm on her microphone and gently pushed it down and out of my way. "I'm sorry, who are you, and what are you doing on my porch?"

'Adina' held the microphone down at her waist and leaned into whisper. "I'm trying to get a good soundbite for the podcast! Just say something very dramatic!" She lifted the microphone again and nodded eagerly.

"I think Beyonce is just *okay*?" I said. I couldn't think of a more provocative statement if I tried. Adina's eyes went wide with that strange fangirl fury, she put the microphone down and turned off her recorder. "Dude, seriously? I can't put that on my podcast! People will rake you over the coals, and me!"

"You asked for something dramatic," I said. "Listen… *Adina Lopez.* Why are you on my porch, and why are you so convinced I'm going to be on your podcast?"

"Uh because I just hooked you up," Adina said blankly. "Didn't you get my email? Old cold case with a six-figure reward. It's right up your alley, and it's on the island!"

"Wait the email was from you?"

"Yeah, didn't you read it?!"

"I literally *just* got it."

Adina giggled. "Yeah, maybe I'm a little hot on the trigger. Could I come in? We can talk, and I can tell you all about the case. Trust me Miss Sponks, you're going to love it!"

"I suppose I don't see the harm in—" I paused. The last person I made friends with turned out to be a murdering lunatic, I couldn't afford to make that mistake again, especially with the Brewdock witches running around the island in secret. I blinked to activate my witch sight, something that let me see magic, and saw nothing coming from Adina. She was as mortal as they come. "Alright, I'll bite. You have ten minutes to catch my interest."

I stepped to the side and Adina cackled with excitement as she stepped inside. "Ha! I only need three!"

CHAPTER 2

As soon as I closed the door Adina stepped in, hit the button on her recorder again and held the clunky microphone to her mouth, walking around my hallway and talking to herself as she did so.

"The home of an amateur investigator is a sight to behold, especially one belonging to a young woman on a mystery solving streak! Although currently unknown on a wider scale, Pendle Island's Chelsea Sponks is quickly rising through the ranks to be known as a sleuth extraordinaire! With over half a dozen successful cases now to her name it's easy to see that Chelsea Sponks is on a one-woman-mission to answer the unanswered, whether she—"

"Adina," I said, clearing my throat to get her attention. Adina paused her recorder.

"Yes?"

"What are you doing?"

"Just recording a first impression of the house. Setting the scene. Painting a description with words." Without waiting for me to respond she hit the button on her recorder again and continued talking. "The house is a charming little thing. A three-story Victorian with a wraparound porch and a large entrance hall. There's charm and character in these walls, and I can imagine our amateur sleuth Chelsea pacing the corridors late at night as she tries to puzzle things out in her mind."

"I literally don't think I've ever done that actually," I said. Adina stopped her recorder again and smiled at me genially.

"Am I overstepping my bounds here?" she asked, looking genuinely oblivious as to why I had stopped her.

"Just a smidgen. Why don't we go into the kitchen, and we'll look at this email, yeah?"

Adina tucked away her recorder and followed me into the kitchen. As I walked in, I made sure to announce that she was human. Loudly. "This is Adina. She's a real nice gal," I said. We hadn't set up a particular code or anything, but Artemis and Lizzy would know from my deliberate tone of voice that Adina wasn't a witch.

The great thing about that meant that Artemis couldn't talk.

"Oh, hi!" Lizzy said cordially from the table. "I'm Chelsea's cousin, Lizzy, and this is her cat, Artemis."

Straightaway Adina pulled out her microphone and started recording again. "I walk into the kitchen where I find Lizzy, one of Chelsea's closest friends and companions. Lizzy is a thimble of a woman, but she has this punk energy to her that hints at something much more ferocious under her delicate exterior. The kitchen is old, the cabinets hanging at odd angles. An old black cat sits on the table, an unspoken simpleness in its green eyes—"

"Uh, what is she doing?" Lizzy said to me.

"She is narrating," I said helplessly, sitting down at the kitchen table, motioning for Adina to do the same. I opened my laptop and clicked on the email.

"Narrating what?" Lizzy said, directing this at Adina. Adina was currently bent over a kettle, describing it fading metallic sheen in great detail to her microphone.

"She's uh one of those podcast types," I said. "She's the one that just sent me the email about the cold-case with a six-figure reward."

"Ah… I see," Lizzy said, still watching Adina in confusion. "Do lots of people listen to podcasts about kitchen roll?" she asked as Adina picked up a kitchen roll and started describing it at length.

"You don't?" I joked.

"I just thought people narrated that kind of scene-setting filler *after the fact*," Lizzy remarked.

"Me too, but something tells me Adina isn't closely acquainted with the word normal."

"Well, you two should get on like a house on fire then," Lizzy laughed. I rolled my eyes at my cousin and cleared my throat to get Adina's attention once more.

"Ahem, hello? Adina?" She paused her recorder again and looked at me. "Remember when I said to chill with the narrating?"

"Oh, yes," she said, chuckling nervously to herself as she put her recorder away. "Sorry, I get carried away." Adina took a seat at the table. "I tend to talk to myself when I'm anxious."

"What are you anxious about?" Lizzy asked.

"Oh everything. New people, new faces, new situations."

"Podcasting seems like an interesting vocational choice then," I commented.

"Yeah, it's a doozy!" she laughed, a little too loudly. "But uh my compulsion to record when I'm anxious means I end up putting out a lot of content. I've only been doing this for a few years, but I've picked up quite a following in that time."

"We don't really have the internet connection out here for podcasts," Lizzy said. "We're a bit behind the times."

"Oh! Well, this is me," Adina said, taking out two business cards and sliding them across the table to each of us. On it there was a picture of Adina, the words 'Fools n' Ghouls' and underneath a subtitle 'The Internet's #1 True Crime Podcast.'

"Number one? In terms of what?" Lizzy asked.

"Uh, listeners… sponsorships… revenue… stadium tours… you name it!" Adina laughed nervously.

Lizzy and I shared a silent glance and then Lizzy let out a long whistle. "So, you're like one of those zillionaire millennials?"

"Something like that!" Adina said, chuckling anxiously again. "Anyway, I was hoping we could talk about the case. You're probably wondering why I'm here, and even how I found your house."

"Eh honestly you'd be surprised how many strange people turn up at my door. Let's just cut to the chase shall we. What's this case about?" I clicked on the email, and it opened. To my surprise there was no body to the email, the only words were in the header. "It's uh… blank," I said.

"Yeah, I figured I'd just deliver the good stuff in person!" Adina snorted. "So, what do you want to know?"

"Why don't you start at the beginning and go from there?" I asked. "Seems like the most logical way of doing it."

Adina gave me a steely nod of approval and then slyly pulled out her recorder again. "As I talk to Chelsea I'm overwhelmed by her clear and precise manner. From the moment you meet her you can hear the cogs whirring away in her mind, sorting information, processing facts, putting everything into its proper box. She's almost cold and robotic, but behind those eyes there is a warmth that reminds you of a strong leader. She's Rosie the Riveter, she's—"

"Adina," I said, pulling her back to focus.

"Sorry!" she laughed, putting the recorder away again.

"Do I really come across like that?" I asked, reflecting on Adina's latest description of me. It was so weird to hear someone narrate me like that.

"Pretty spot on I'd say," Lizzy remarked.

I let out a deflated sigh. "This is very weird for me."

"Okay so have you ever heard of Declan King?" Adina asked.

"No," I said and shook my head

"I have," Lizzy said. "Dec King, the decking king! Discount decks at delightful prices!" I stared at Lizzy, and she flustered. "What? Those ads used to play like a hundred times a day when I was growing up."

"Then you probably heard about the big court case he was involved in?" Adina asked.

"Oh sure. Killed his wife and he got away with it due to a technicality. I remember when that happened a few years ago. It was wild!"

"That really happened?" I asked Adina, prompting her for more information.

"It was a dark and stormy night," Adina said hitting her recorder again. I sighed and wondered how long this was going to take exactly. "The quiet rock that is Pendle Island is a thirty-minute flight from Los Angeles, a small shield of mountainous rock standing tall against the ferocious power of the Pacific Ocean…"

"She's good!" Lizzy whispered, leaning over to me to convey her approval of Adina's atmospheric scene setting.

"Its capital town isn't home to more than a few thousand permanent residents, one of whom is Declan King, a self-titled 'king' of decking and home improvements. For years Dec ran a successful hardware store, and through his decking business he amassed a small fortune in the millions. Life was good until one night his wife, Meredith King, was found dead in their hilltop mansion."

"Okay Adina let's pause a moment," I said, jumping in at a natural breathing space. Adina did hit pause. "Can you tell me about the case without narrating it to me? This is a very weird way to receive information."

"Sorry, force of habit. Basically, Meredith was bludgeoned to death in her home. It was a forced entry, looked like a break-in gone wrong, or at least was *made* to look like that."

"So, people think her husband, this Dec King, he killed her and tried to make it look like a robbery?"

Adina nodded. "He was the only other person with access to the property. He got dragged through the courts, and it wasn't looking good for him, but he got off."

"How?"

"The prosecution messed up some paperwork and a bunch of stuff wasn't admissible in court. Dec basically got a get out a jail free card. He still has the hardware shop in town but it's not nearly as busy these days, his younger brother runs the shop. Dec still lives on the island, but he's become something of a recluse."

"Okay, and what about this reward, who's offering that?"

"That's from Dec himself," Adina said.

"Wait, what?" I asked. I hadn't expected that.

"Yup, to this day he maintains his innocence, though half the people on the island have him down as the killer. He put up the reward recently. Said he wants to move on and put the past behind him."

I blinked, soaking up the information. "What do you think?" I said and looked at Lizzy.

"I mean I always thought he was guilty. That guy has a weird energy about him."

"Why offer up a reward though if he's guilty?" I asked.

"It casts doubt," Lizzy surmised. "If he *did* do it, then there's no way a person could solve otherwise. Makes him look innocent."

That it did indeed.

"I have to admit that I'm intrigued, but I'm curious now Adina, how did you hear about this case? And why do you bring it to me?" I asked her.

"The case came to me from one of my listeners actually. I've been meaning to come to Pendle Island for a while, I mean this place is like mecca for paranormal activity. I cover a lot of that stuff on my podcast too. Wednesday is Whacky Wednesdays, where I cover unexplained phenomenon. Anyway, I started looking into Pendle Island and I saw your face on a few of the recent front pages. As soon as I saw your face, I knew you were the one for this case. I mean, it's a match made in heaven!"

"You don't say. Who was your listener?"

Adina shrugged. "I don't remember. I have an inbox for episode suggestions, and I just plucked something out of there. I wouldn't be surprised if I have a few fans on this island. I hope it's not too much trouble, but while I'm on the island I think I'd like to follow you around while you work on this case—"

"I haven't even accepted it yet, what makes you think I'm going to take it?"

Adina smiled. "You really want to know what I think?"

"...Yes."

She picked up her microphone again and hit record. I should

have known better. "So, I sit in the kitchen of Chelsea Sponks' house, this curious amateur investigator. I tell her all about the case and then I notice something. A change comes over her. Her fingers start tapping on the table. She crosses her legs and taps her feet. She's looking at me, and she's more than polite, but there's a distance in her eyes, I can tell this mystery is already consuming her, she—"

"Alright that's enough," I said, feeling wigged out again to hear my every movement narrated back to me.

"She *is* good!" Lizzy chuckled. "I can see why you're number one."

"So, what do you say?" Adina asked. "Can I follow you around? There're a few other things I want to check out while I'm here on the island. Apparently, there's some wicked witch scene here."

I gulped. "Witches?"

"Yeah, this is like a big pagan scene, isn't it? You both strike me as the type."

"Oh, pagan," I said, laughing nervously. "Yeah. We're both big pagans. Go witches!"

Adina coughed awkwardly. "Anyway... there's quite a bit on this island to keep me interested, and something tells me there's no better escort than you Chelsea Sponks. You seem to be a pivotal figure around here at the moment!"

"I don't know about that," I said modestly.

"You should see her recent track record," Lizzy said. "Twenty-five missing animal cases in two weeks."

Adina's brows raised in intrigue. "Amateur sleuth *and* pet detective? Color me intrigued."

"I'm *not* a pet detective," I said adamantly. "I was just clearing out some old emails. There's been a lull of activity at the moment, and I'm trying to scrape together a bit of money anyway."

"Oh?" Adina asked. "Any particular reason?"

"Just... getting my expenses in order," I said. I didn't exactly feel like sharing pregnancy news with a perfect stranger at the moment. I still hadn't told anyone else apart from Deacon and Artemis.

"Well say no more!" Adina said. "I'm quite happy to reimburse you for your time." Adina took out a pen and pad, scribbled something down and pushed it over to me. "What do you say to that?"

I looked down at the pad, upon which Adina had written '$1000'. "Adina that is very generous of you, but it seems there's already enough reward money at stake for this old case. Another thousand isn't necessary."

"I think you're confused," Adina said. "That's what I'm offering as a day rate, every day until I leave. I follow you around and see what happens, and maybe you indulge me every now and then. So, what do you say?"

My mouth dropped at hearing the words 'day rate'. I looked over at Lizzy and saw her equally shocked. "Well Adina… I'd say welcome to Pendle Island! Would you like to stay in the guest room?"

CHAPTER 3

*A*fter that it was pretty much settled in my mind that Adina was going to be staying here for a few days while I gave her a tour of the island. The guest room in the house was now free since Selena had moved out, so I did have the space to accommodate someone. Adina certainty seemed like she was a bit of a wildcard, but she didn't strike me as the type to staple teabags to skirting boards, so I figured it would be less stressful than having Selena around.

"Okay, I'm all unpacked!" Adina said cheerily as she came bounding down the stairs twenty minutes later.

"That was… quick," I remarked, sipping a cup of tea while I read the paper.

"Well, I'm keen to hit the road and get going!" Adina said with a bright smile. She walked across the kitchen and scratched Artemis behind the ears. "What's happening in the paper today?" she asked.

"A whole lot of nothing. I mean, they've taken to printing the conspiracy nut business, so you can tell it's a slow news day."

Adina pulled out her microphone straightaway and I held my breath in anticipation. As I was kind of a temporary employee of Adina's now, I had to be a little more patient of her recording habit. "Newspapers, they're funny things…" she began. "Ink on paper, black on white. Reflections of the stories around us, an inanimate object that can move us, inform us, even… *change* us. A relic lost to the tides of technology, I argue the newspaper still has its place and purpose in our digital world. Everyone wants to be the headline, but one thing is for sure… we all make the obituary page." Adina clicked the recorder off and looked at me. "Too pretentious?"

"A little bit. I like it though. How long do these podcast episodes normally last?"

"Oh, I edit down *a lot*. The main episodes I put out run for about an hour or two, but then I do my *B-Sides* as well, I guess you could call it extra footage. Those can run for hours."

"And people listen to that?" I asked in surprise. How did people even find the time?

"Oh yeah, for sure. Some of my most hardcore fans even set up a forum to talk about my podcast. I don't venture there much myself, usually too busy recording!"

"I see that. Well, there's certainly enough on this island to keep you occupied. How do you make money with this by the way? Do people buy episodes or what?"

"Not quite. The main podcast is free, but I have sponsorships, subscriptions, merchandise, live shows… you name it."

"A lot of people sponsor this kind of thing?"

"Oh yeah, I have about fifty million regular listeners, so I get all sorts of sponsorship requests. My main sponsor at the moment is Alpaca Wool Socks!" Adina put on an advertising voice. "Soft, warm, eco-friendly, put your feet in something neat!" Adina broke out of the voice and laughed.

"Sign me up," I joked.

"You want some? I've got like two hundred pairs in the back of my van…for real. As well as sponsorships I have direct subscribers. People have to subscribe to my premium feed for the B-Side episodes, it's only a dollar a month."

"And how many people do that?" I asked out of curiousness.

"Last time I checked I think it was about thirty thousand?" she said, though she didn't seem sure of the number.

"Holy moly!" I said, my eyes going wide. "I guess crime really *does* pay."

Adina laughed. "I guess so!" She looked back at the newspaper. "What's this about conspiracy nut business then?" Adina asked. I turned the newspaper around so she could see the double-spread story I was reading. It was a story about a curator at the Pendle Museum, convinced that the items in the collection had been replaced with forgeries. There was a picture of the curator, a young man named Zack, pointing his thumb at a wall of Egyptian artifacts and pulling a funny face. A huge headline next to the story read: *King Tut-tut-tut! Are mummy artifacts fake?!*

"Huh, cutting edge news," Adina joked.

"Yeah. Actually, I think this guy messaged me asking for help. I ignored it."

"Not your cup of tea?" Adina asked me, pulling the paper in to get a closer look.

"I mean it's not that, I just don't know the first thing about Egyptian artifacts. It's got nothing to do with me." Solving murders and identifying ancient artifacts were two completely different things. I was *not* the gal for that.

"This type of thing is right up my street actually," Adina said. "My listeners love a good conspiracy. Do you think we could swing around the museum and talk to this guy, see what he has to say?"

My first instinct was to say no, but then I remembered that I had agreed to be Adina's guide of the island, and in exchange I would be paid handsomely for my time. "Let's make an arrangement, if I'm going to be your guide to the island then we'll try and split the time equally. Each day we do stuff I want to do, and stuff that you want to do too. Deal?"

"Deal!" Adina said excitedly. "By my watch we've got several hours of sunlight left for today, so what are you proposing?"

"I want to run down to the hardware store and see if I can talk to this Declan King character. I still haven't decided if the case is for me yet, but once I talk to him, I'll be able to make up my mind."

"Sounds great!" Adina sang. "How about after that you take me to the museum, and we can get check out this artifact business?"

I wasn't exactly thrilled about indulging this museum thread, but I had to admit there was a small part of me that wanted to hear the story. "Okay, you strike a hard bargain Adina. I can drive if you want, my little yellow buttercup is small and rusty, but she sure is reliable!"

"Oh, we can take my ride, I parked it around the side," Adina said.

"What do you drive?" I asked.

Adina grinned. "Come on, I'll show you."

We both left the house and I followed Adina around to the side, where I saw a large van painted with black and purple streaks. On the roof just above the front window there was a large fiberglass skull with roses coming out of its eyes. On the side of the van were the words 'Fouls n' Ghouls' painted in big wavy letters. I didn't know the first thing about vans, but this thing looked expensive.

"Cream on a cracker, it's the mystery machine!" I said in amazement.

"She's my pride and beauty!" Adina beamed. "Had to pay one heck of a fee to get her ferried out here, but I don't go anywhere without Betsy, she's my good luck omen. And she's got AC!"

"Don't tell my little yellow buttercup, but I think I've found a new love," I said, climbing into the van with Adina. We both buckled up and Adina put the directions into her phone. "Ooh this is exciting, the first waypoint on my adventure of Pendle Island! After coming to your house of course."

"My house was your first stop after arriving here?"

Adina nodded. "Of course, I wanted to get down to business straightaway. The old man that flew me over here was more than happy to let me know where you live!"

"Smithy?" I said, recalling the mustachioed geriatric that had flown me over to the island. "I'll have to have a word with him about being so free with my personal info."

"Oh, don't give him a hard time, I lied and said I was your long-lost cousin. He seemed very enamored by the idea, plus his wife is a fan of the podcast apparently. I gave him some merch in return."

"Everyone has their price, eh?" I laughed. "Let's hit the road then, time to pay…" I looked at the name of the hardware store and glanced at Adina. "Fort Fix It? Really?"

"Hey, don't look at me, I didn't name the place. This is your town. You haven't been to the hardware store before?"

"My friend Adam takes care of all the house stuff. I haven't set foot in a hardware store in—" I paused and thought about it. "Actually, I've never been to a hardware store before. Am I missing out?"

"Big time," Adina said in a joking way. "Buckle up. You're in for a wild afternoon."

CHAPTER 4

Ten minutes later we pulled up in the center of town. I was familiar with most of the town now and knew most of its businesses, but I had to confess that 'Fort Fix It' wasn't somewhere I had come across so far on my travels.

We were at a strip mall, and right at the far end there was a huge cinderblock warehouse with the words 'Fort Fix It' hanging in massive yellow letters above the entrance. The other businesses in this strip mall were in equally large buildings, with similarly obnoxious sized signs: *Pet Barn, Food DEPOT, Sport Factory,* and more. It appeared this part of town was set aside for these huge multi-national businesses that cropped up everywhere, cinderblock fortresses that cast a shadow over the small local businesses in town—literally and figuratively.

"Didn't think I'd find something like this on Pendle Island," Adina remarked as we walked towards the hardware store. "I thought it was a sleepy town with mom-and-pop businesses."

"It is for the most part, the parking lot looks pretty empty if you ask me, looks like a lot of the locals still prefer shopping local. I know the island council had budget issues a few years ago, they sold off quite a lot off land to big businesses to balance their sheets. This strip mall was a result of that I think."

Adina opened her mouth as if she was going to respond but I saw her pull out her microphone. She started talking, slipping into another bout of narration. "Pendle Island is a charming place for the most part, an unusual jewel hidden off the western coast of the states. Pendle town is a quiet town, a place where everyone seems to know everyone, and hospitality is available in spades. Still even at the edge of the world parts of Pendle Island seem unable to escape the capitalist titans that have dwarfed the smaller businesses of middle America. We walk through the parking lot of a strip mall to *Fort Fix It*, the business owned by Declan King, our supposed murderer that got off on a technicality."

Adina paused the recording and lowered her microphone.

"Man, you can really just turn that on whenever you want, huh?" I asked, referring to her narrating.

"You should step inside my brain for a moment and listen. My thoughts never shut off. Getting them onto tape helps calm my mind, though only a little. Even as I'm talking to you now my brain is narrating like five different topics at once."

I grimaced. "Sounds like you've got a lot going on up there."

"You have no idea."

The automatic doors of the hardware store opened on our approach, and we walked inside. 'Store' probably wasn't the right word, we were essentially in a massive warehouse, its aisles made up of gargantuan steel shelves. Elevator music played casually over the store, and as we walked in there was a large carboard cutout of a man dressed as a cowboy, a lasso in the air above him.

"High Prices no more! Permanent Lasso discount! 30% off for all club members!"

Despite the size of the store there weren't any other customers in here at the moment. I couldn't even see a member of staff.

"That's the guy, right?" I asked Adina, recognizing the huge cutout as Declan King from the little bit of research I'd conducted before coming over here. In the photos I had seen Mr. King looked smart and well-kept, a silver-haired businessman in his fifties, cosmetically whitened teeth, bright blue eyes and a tan from the bottle. The cutout was similar, except for the ridiculous cowboy getup.

"Yeah that's 'Dec King', he rebranded himself after the court case, wanted to put as much distance between himself and the murder as possible," Adina said. "He now calls himself the 'Handmade Honcho', he's really leaning into it."

"The cowboy theme seems a bold choice for a hardware store," I laughed. I guess the macho appeal of ten-gallon-hats and spurs outweighed the negative connotations of being a cowboy tradesman for Mr. King.

"So, what do we do first?" Adina asked. "I'm new to this side of things. Normally I'm only reporting about mysteries after the fact, I've never been involved in the investigative side of things before."

I pursed my lips as I tried to get my bearings on the situation. Right now, I was standing in a hardware store owned by a suspected murderer, but beyond that I didn't have much leverage to solve anything. "I suppose we go and find someone, see if the Honcho himself is in."

We walked up to a customer service desk, and I rang a bell. Almost an entire minute passed before a balding and out of breath man appeared from a door that led into the back. He was wearing a shirt and tie. "Sorry about the delay, just trying to unload a shipment in the back! How can I help you?"

I opened my mouth to speak but Adina got there first, her microphone poised at her lips. "'Fort Fix It' is a sparse cinderblock desert, shelves of galvanized steel holding endless sheets of lumber and power tools. The bright halogen lights overhead make everything feel cold, and the grey concrete floors remind me of a desert devoid of any life. A balding man with a paunch is our first contact at an abandoned customer service station. He has dark rings under his eyes and he's red in the face."

The balding man stared back at Adina in bewilderment as she put her microphone back down and paused her recorded. "Uh... what?" he asked. "Are you reporters?"

"No—" I began, but once again Adina stepped in.

"Adina Lopez," Adina said, extending a card to the gentleman behind the desk. "I host Fools n' Ghouls, the internet's preeminent true crime podcast."

"Oh, I've heard of you guys, my daughter listens to the show." He looked at the card then back at us, an uncertain look on his face. "Look if you're here to talk about the business with Declan and the case, we've got nothing for you, I'm sorry but I'll have to ask you to—"

"Actually, I'm here to inquire about the reward," I said. "Apparently Mr. King has just offered up a $100k incentive to prove his innocence."

The man behind the counter stared at me for a moment, an expression I had come to learn recently as my own celebrity on the island grew. "Wait a minute I know you! You're that girl that solves the crimes! The amateur sleuth!"

I held my hands jokingly, like a thief caught in the act. "You got me. My friend Adina here made me aware of the offering from Mr. King, I was hoping if I could speak to him and perhaps find out a little more about the case."

"Of course, of course!" he said excitedly. "Oh, Dec's gonna be thrilled to hear that you want in on this. My name's Bryan by the way, I'm Dec's younger brother. From all accounts you're a certified pro! Let me call him now and see if I can find out where he—"

"Watching Chelsea work is a fascinating affair," Adina began, completely oblivious that she was talking over our conversation. "It's almost like there are two halves to her brain, the quiet unassuming regular Chelsea, and the mystery hungry machine that lurks underneath. Once she jumps into action there's no mistaking it, she'll bite down and won't let go until she gets what she wants, like a rabid—"

"Um, Adina?" I said, clearing my throat to get her attention. She paused and snapped out of her trance-like focus.

"Yes?" she asked.

"Excuse me one second, Bryan. Adina, can we have a word for a moment, over here?" I placed my hand softly on Adina's arm and walked a few paces away from the service desk.

"What's up?" she whispered, leaning in close and looking back at the desk. "Is it the balding guy? Have you seen something? Do you think he's the killer?!"

"Um, no, I only just got the guy's name, even I don't work that fast. We've got a little problem, and it's you."

"Me?" Adina said in confusion.

"Yeah, the constant recording and the interruptions, it's kind of messing with my flow a little bit."

Adina grimaced apologetically, letting a long breath out through her braced teeth. "Sorry, I've heard that before. I'm just excited to be in the thick of things!"

"Right, I get that, but I don't think we're going to get to the bottom of anything if you're recording narration every thirty seconds. How about we split up for a little bit? You can wander the store—or the strip mall—and get some footage for your *B-sides*. In the meantime, I'm free to do my own thing. We can meet back up in a bit."

"I think it's a brilliant idea," Adina said. "Twice the coverage, half the effort."

"What?" I said.

Adina pulled out a handheld recorded and passed it to me. "Take this. If you speak to anyone ask if they're okay with being recorded for the podcast—get their consent on tape. Record everything! I'm sure you're going to get gold! Gold!"

Before I could even protest Adina was off, walking down an aisle and recording more narration. "I cruise down an aisle full of large paint cans, each one closed, their dark contents sealed within. In a way the unspoken truths that surround us are similar, secrets hidden in shadowy vessels, lost until..."

Adina disappeared around a corner, her verbose and unending narration fading from my ear. I let out a measured breath and walked back to Bryan at the desk.

"Sorry about that," I said. "She's... keen. Did you say you can get me a conversation with your brother?"

"I'll give him a call now," Bryan said. "You wait right here." With that Bryan disappeared once again through the door that led into the back, this time leaving the door slightly ajar as he went through. I stood there for a few seconds, tapping my foot on the ground as I waited.

Bryan had barely been gone all of thirty seconds when the urge to sneak into the back overwhelmed me.

"Ah, what the heck," I muttered under my breath, my mind tracing back to an invisibility spell that I had come across in a book a few days ago while studying magic. I looked around quickly to make sure no one could see me—I didn't exactly want to vanish into thin air in front of regular mortals—and then I whispered the incantation to myself. *"Lux vertere Umbra!"*

The change came over me at once, a pool of rippling magic that flowed down from the crown of my head, right down to the soles of my feet. It was a warm and shimmering tide, and from my perspective I saw a translucent blue coat of magic flickering over my body. To everyone else I was completely invisible.

There were several different ways to make oneself invisible with magic, but I'd chosen this one as it used the least magic, meaning I could stay invisible for longer. Magic didn't exactly come with a fuel gauge, but every witch had an innate sense of how much power she had remaining.

I could tell with this spell active I had about ten minutes of invisibility until my powers would be completely spent—not too shabby. The only drawback of the spell is that any sound I made wouldn't be cloaked. I still had to be careful about sneaking around unless I wanted to draw undue attention to myself.

With my invisibility active I ducked behind the customer service counter and slipped through the door that led into the back. I found myself in a room that seemed to be both an office and a storage area. There were a few desks with computers, but only one was currently occupied. Sitting there was Bryan, the man I had just been speaking with at the desk.

"Yeah, the girl from the papers, the egghead! I'm telling you, Dec, she's here clear as day! If anyone can get you out of this fix it's her!" Bryan paused as he waited for a response from the other end of the call. Even with my invisibility I couldn't eavesdrop the other end of a phone call. I could heighten my hearing with magic, but this invisibility spell was already pretty taxing stuff. "Sure, I'll pass it on to her. Look while I've got you on the phone, I was hoping I could—" Bryan paused and put the phone onto speaker, he set the handset back on the desk while he taped up some parcels that were on his desk. "Listen I wanted to talk to you about those informercials I proposed the other day, I really think they could help pick the business up, and lord knows we need it Dec—"

"Bryan," came Declan's voice from the speaker, "What did I say about this? I pay you to work, not to think. I've got enough on my plate as it is, I don't need any more of your harebrained schemes."

"But Dec, we've got to change something or we're going to go under. I think a few adverts would really—"

"How many times do I have to say this? I'm the rich one. I'm the successful one. If your ideas were worth anything then it'd be your face out there swinging the giant cardboard lasso. Now are we done here?"

Bryan let out a long and frustrated sigh. I couldn't imagine it would be easy living in the shadow of a successful brother, especially one that talked to him like that. "Sure."

"Good, can you put me on with Susan really quick? I want to talk to her about those inventory reports. Oh, before I forget Jennifer should be there any minute."

"I didn't realize she was in today," Bryan commented.

"Well, you know what she's like. She does her own thing."

"Let me find Susan." Bryan picked up the phone and walked out of the room, heading down a long corridor before knocking at an open door of a small office. I followed close behind, holding my breath as I walked.

"I'm busy," a voice came from in the office.

"It's Declan," Bryan replied. "He's on the phone and wants to speak to you."

"Very well," said an ashy blonde woman working at a desk. She took the phone and waited for Bryan to leave, I remained, watching in silence. Once he left, she spoke. "These inventory reports are hell Declan; I don't know how you expect me to get through them before the tax year is over."

"Enough about that," Declan's voice responded over the speaker. "Jennifer is coming in, she's going to ask for money, you need to tell her there isn't any."

"What? Why am I the last line of defense! She's your wife, you tell her!"

"Just cover my butt, will you?" Declan asked over the phone. "I've not got the energy to deal with her today."

Susan rolled her eyes and huffed. Something told me she'd been put in this position before. "Very well, but this is the last time. You know things would have been a whole lot easier if you'd just married me instead," she said. Susan phrased it as a joke, but I could tell there was a layer of sincerity underneath her humor. There was no ring on her finger.

Declan glossed over the comment completely. "Thanks Susan, you're the best." Without another word the line went dead. Susan pursed her lips and turned the phone over. "That woman will be the death of him," she muttered to herself.

I slipped out of the room and headed back to the office behind the customer service desk. Only on my way back did I notice a bank of surveillance screens, one of them pointing down at the customer service desk I had just been standing at. *Oh... drat!*

I'd just performed magic on camera!

"Think, Chelsea, think!" I whispered to myself, looking around frantically as though the answer would be here somewhere in this room. I didn't know the first thing about surveillance units like this and had no idea how I was supposed to wipe the footage. *A spot of magic might take care of it though.*

I waved my hand over the terminal and muttered a spell to myself to clear the footage away. The incantation I was focusing on was very simple, a magnetic chaos that would render the unit useless. Perhaps a little excessive, but the only answer I could think of in a quick pinch.

The monitors on the unit clicked off and I knew I'd successfully taken care of that problem. I was about to head back to the desk when Bryan came back into the room, following the heels of an extravagant looking blonde woman who looked like she was no stranger to a spa day. "I'm just saying," Bryan said in a hushed tone. "I'm here for you if you ever want to talk. Declan doesn't give you the respect you deserve, after everything he's put you through, Jennifer!"

"I'm fine Bryan, honestly," Jennifer said with an air of indifference. "Now can you be a doll and help me out with this one thing? Susan's already said no, Dec must have called ahead and warned her. I'm short on cash and my corporate card is strapped. Can I borrow a little from yours?"

"Again?" Bryan asked with an uneasy frown.

"I know darling, but we'll make it all square come next month, I promise. Come on, you know I'm always good for it. Where's the checkbook, in here?" Jennifer had a tone of someone that didn't know, but she went straight over to Bryan's desk and found his checkbook in the first drawer she looked in. She pulled it out and started writing a check to herself. Bryan stood there on the sideline, like a helpless puppy.

Jennifer tore the check out of the book and held it up so Bryan could see. "What do you think? Is that a satisfiable amount? Not too much."

"It's fine," Bryan mumbled, "Except for one thing." He took the check out of Jennifer's hands, placed it on the table and made an adjustment. "My name is Bryan with a 'Y', not and 'I'. Why can you never remember that? How long have we worked together, and you always get it wrong."

Jennifer just laughed as she took the check out of Bryan's hands. "Bryan you're a darling, it's not my fault you spell your name so silly."

"Everyone else gets it right," he grumbled.

"Now excuse me, Bryan, I've got things to do and places to be," Jennifer said as she waltzed out of the office. Bryan watched her leave, shook his head and brushed a hand through his balding hair. "You're a damn idiot, Bryan," he said to himself.

I realized then that Bryan was very likely heading back to the customer service desk, so I sprinted out of the room, slipped through the open door and appeared on the other side of the counter, ending my invisibility spell as I did so. Bryan came back through the door a moment later, I pretended to be surprised and smiled. "I was starting to think you weren't coming back!" I joked.

Bryan looked confused. "I just came out here a second ago and you were gone."

Oops. "Oh, I was looking at that paint over there. Did you get hold of your brother?"

"I did. Declan wants to talk to you, but he's not coming down to the shop." Bryan handed me a folded piece of paper. "That's his address and contact number. He wants to meet you at his house. Just call ahead of time to make sure he's available. Should be, he just sits at home drinking all day," Bryan muttered, mostly to himself.

"Uh thanks!" I said. "Well, I better get going. I might come back to talk some more!"

"Yeah, yeah," Bryan said dismissively, waving me away as he headed into the back again. With my first bout of sleuthing done I wandered through the aisles of the store until I found Adina in the gardening section at the back, talking to herself while she looked over a tray of succulents.

"…but that perhaps is the greatest mystery of all. Life prevails even in the face of—Chelsea!" Adina stood up and stopped recording. "Are you done already?"

"I think so, Dec's given me the greenlight to talk to him, and I've dug up a few things here already I think."

"Ooh, anything juicy?" Adina said, holding her microphone up to no doubt catch another juicy soundbite.

"Let's talk in the van, it's more private." I paused and looked at the succulents. "Still recording for your B-sides?"

"I just really like succulents. I had a podcast about them too, but it didn't do as well."

"I wonder why," I said humorously. "Come on, let's head back to the van. We've got stuff to go over!"

CHAPTER 5

"So," Adina said keenly as we pulled out of the parking lot. "What have we learned so far?"

"That man at the customer service desk, Bryan, he's Declan's younger brother. After he went into the back I snuck in there after him and eavesdropped a few conversations."

"Woah!" Adina said, looking visibly impressed. "How did you do that?"

I shrugged and smiled. "Let's just say you get good at sneaking around after a while." Magic helped too, but Adina couldn't know about that.

"What did you overhear then?" she asked me.

"Bryan was on the phone to his brother, after he finished talking about me, he brought up informercials."

"Infomercials?" Adina asked.

"Yeah, it seems like Bryan is quite keen to get some new informercials filmed for the hardware store to try and drum up a little business. He put the idea to Dec, but he shot it down."

"Tough break I guess," Adina mused. She turned the van right and headed into town. At the moment we didn't have a destination, she was just driving for fun.

"Maybe. It sounded like this was something Bryan had brought up a few times before, and his brother, Dec, didn't exactly shoot it down in the nicest way. I get the feeling Bryan is a little downtrodden, living in the shadow of his more successful brother."

Adina's eyes suddenly sparkled with the promise of intrigue. "Wait a minute, you think this Bryan guy might be a suspect?!"

"What? I never said that."

"No, but you're thinking it, I can tell!" she said. "Maybe the downtrodden brother killed his sister-in-law to get back at his brother. Maybe they were having an affair and he killed her before she went public with it!"

"Can you tell me what you know about the case, starting from scratch?" I asked Adina.

"Right, I guess I never actually ran the full case properly past you. Dec King and his wife Gloria had this big, gated house up in the hills overlooking the town. On the night of the murder, she was in the house alone. A broken window around the side of the house suggested forced entry, but apart from that there were no other clues. No other suspects apart from Dec."

"Well, it seems that Bryan has a strained relationship with his brother, but Bryan *is* also working there at the shop, so things can't be all that bad. I also overheard a phone call with Dec and his secretary, Susan."

"Man, you really are good at this sneaking around stuff, eh?" Adina asked. "What did you hear on the call?"

"Dec's wife Jennifer was coming into the shop to ask for money, he called ahead of the time to tell the secretary to say no," I answered.

"Ah… so he can't say no to his wife, but he's making his secretary do it."

"Something like that. I also feel like the secretary has old feelings for her boss, she made a joke that he should have married her instead. And get this, back in the office I heard Bryan talking with Dec's wife. Something tells me *he's* got feelings for her too."

"Man, you were only in there five minutes, and you've already found a whole heap of mess. How did you do all that without getting caught? You had to be invisible!"

I laughed nervously looked out the window. "I'm pretty good at blending in with the background scenery I guess."

"What now then?" Adina asked.

"Let's see what Declan has to say," I said, pulling out the folded note that Bryan had handed to me. Upon it was a phone number and address for his brother. I pulled out my phone and dialed the number. It rang seven times before anyone answered.

"Hello?" came a gruff voice.

"Hi, this is Chelsea Sponks, is that Dec King?"

"The one and only," Dec said after another long pause. The slur on his voice told me that he was more than a little drunk. "Bryan called. He told me you were sniffing around. Says you can prove my innocence."

"Well, I don't know about that, but I'm certainly interested in looking at things a little more closely. I was hoping we could meet and talk. I'd like to get your perspective on things. I'm free now if that works for you."

"No, not now," Dec slurred. "This is my pool time now. I don't let anything disturb that. I'm too wasted to talk anyway. I'll be at Monterey Golf Course tomorrow morning first thing. You can meet me there, eight sharp."

"I'm not much of a golfer," I said.

"I don't care about the golf. You seem like a darn fine sleuth, and that's all that matters to me. See you tomorrow, Miss Sponks."

"See you then."

The call ended and I put my phone back into my pocket. "First thing tomorrow at the golf club. Dec doesn't want to talk now. From the sounds of things, he's at the bottom of a whiskey bottle, floating around a pool."

"Sounds safe!" Adina laughed. "I guess that means the rest of the afternoon is free then. Perhaps you'd be willing to indulge me in something? Remember our arrangement? We split up the day?"

"Sure thing," I nodded. Even though Adina was paying me handsomely for my time she still seemed hesitant about ordering me around. "What were you thinking?"

"I'm thinking I want to check out this Egyptian exhibit at the museum," Adina said with an intrigued grin. "I'm not sure why, the idea of fake artifacts has me all intrigued. Fancy coming along?"

I shrugged. The supposed fake artifacts didn't interest me at all, but I was prepared to act as a guide and help Adina while she was staying here on the island. "Let's do it. I haven't got a fedora or anything, if I'd known we'd be hunting stolen artifacts I would have brought one."

"A fedora?" Adina asked in confusion.

"Like Indiana Jones?" I clarified.

"Oh! Yeah, I've heard of those films. My granddad loved them!"

I sank in my seat and groaned, never having felt older since spending time with someone ten years my junior. "You kids have a great way of making me feel old," I grumbled.

* * *

PENDLE MUSEUM WAS A RATHER extravagant looking building. At the front a wide bank of steps led up to the entrance, a tall set of double doors that were grand and imposing. Large stone pillars ran along on the front on either side of the doors, in between which were stained glass windows.

Upon our approach Adina effortlessly slipped back into her narration. "We approach an old-time museum, a large stone building that wouldn't look out of place in a romantic adventure movie. Beyond its majestic front doors there lies the past, the foundations and building blocks of history from which modern man so boldly strode forward. Somewhere in these corridors of history however another mystery might just lurk. Are there forgeries in this museum, lying in plain sight?" Adina put her microphone down again as we climbed the steps.

"So... do you have family?" I asked. "Where are you from originally?" If I was really going to be spending time with Adina it only seemed polite to get to know her.

"Ever heard of Grentone, Texas?" she asked.

"Uh, no?"

Adina laughed. "You and every other American in the states today. That's my hometown, it's a little middle-of-nowhere town with not much more than fifty people."

"Huh, really out in the sticks then, huh?"

"Don't you know it! Never knew my papa, and I'm the youngest of three by fifteen years. Momma is a nurse, so she was always at work. I was a latchkey kid in a dustbowl town. Only thing I really had for company as a kid was my tape recorder, I guess that's where the passion started."

"The same recorder you use now?" I asked.

"No," Adina laughed. "It was a little plaything, though I still have it on a shelf back in my home studio. I live in LA now. That recorder was my best friend growing up. It's no surprise I'm still talking to one today."

"Do you have a boyfriend, girlfriend, pets?" I asked.

"Four cats," Adina nodded. "My older sister helps look after them when I'm out on the road. Not really interested in doing the whole love thing at the moment, I'm just focusing on my career, striking while the iron is hot and all that jazz. I've never even had a boyfriend. Never even been kissed!"

"Huh," I said. Though it was a little unusual, Adina didn't seem too hung up about it. "Well, you take your time. There's no sense in rushing that type of thing. I'm sure the right person will come along when you're ready."

"And if they don't, I've always got my recorder," Adina grinned.

The automatic glass doors opened, and we headed into the welcoming lobby of the museum. I'd only been here once and that was a few months ago, to oversee an art exhibit that Lizzy was helping with. Naturally a body turned up that night, and I'd been the one to puzzle things out.

A large tyrannosaurus skeleton stood tall in the middle of the lobby, and beyond that there was an antique war plane suspended in the air, above the heads of the few people wandering about. Several large doors led to different themed exhibits, the one immediately to our left was adorned replica Egyptian statues, the bold black archway decorated with bright gold hieroglyphics.

Adina paid our entry and we headed into the exhibit, a series of eight or nine connecting rooms full to the brim with artifacts, replica props, little information cards and animated movies—the whole nine yards.

I had to admit the exhibit was captivating, I found myself caught up in the majesty and the romance of the past, especially a past as extravagant as ancient Egypt. Apart from a few stragglers there weren't really that many people about, so Adina and I were able to lap the exhibit fairly quickly, casually taking in the sights along the way as we ambled around admiring the displays.

The exhibit itself ended in a large room in which a miniature replica pyramid had been built. On the wall behind it there were several large glass display cabinets filled with ancient looking artifacts. Gold armor shimmered under the museum lights, various bronze tools and broken pots and vases delicately put back together. Amongst the shelves of pottery and stone head pieces one cabinet at the center of the wall was the most impressive, inside which there were four distinct tools crafted from bronze or gold—I couldn't quite tell which.

"Ah, you've noticed the jewel of the exhibit then," a young man said as he stepped in beside us. He was wearing a museum polo shirt. "You're looking at the *Adawat of Anubis,* tools the jackal-headed god used when delivering spirits in the afterlife. His ankh is the key of life, the tool that let him walk through the next world. His spear was his defense against evil spirits, his scales let him weigh the hearts of dead kings, and his scepter—well that was perhaps his most powerful item."

"What was his scepter for?" I asked.

"His scepter gave him complete control over whomever was in his company. The god frequently dealt with great and powerful kings, so it was important he had means to keep them at his side, to ensure they didn't stray in the land of dead and get lost on their way to the afterlife."

I looked over at Adina and noticed that she was—of course—recording this impromptu moment with the young man from the museum. It was nice to learn a little about history and all, that much I couldn't dispute.

"If you're both interested, I could give you a tour of the exhibit. Another one is due to start in—wait a minute!" All of sudden the young man stepped back and looked at me in a new light. "It's you! You're the detective girl! Oh man! You got my message!"

"Wait, you're the one that contacted me?" I asked. There had been a request in my inbox, someone claiming the artifacts in the museum were fake.

"That's me, I'm Zack, I work here in the museum!"

"In an interesting twist of fate, it turns out we run right into our lead," Adina said into her microphone. "Zack is a young man, broad shouldered and keen to inform. He's the one that suspects something is afoot at Pendle Museum."

Zack stared at Adina in confusion then looked at me for clarity. "She's a podcaster," I said, as if that explained away her baffling behavior. He nodded as though it did. In fact, he even seemed taken with the idea.

"Oh, excellent! Yes! By all means, we need as much attention on this as possible! Listen, I'm so glad you came down. I didn't think you would!"

"I'm actually here to show Adina around, but I suppose now that I'm here I might as well hear what you have to say. Something about fake artifacts?"

"Fake isn't the word, stolen is more like! There's a sinister plot at work here, a master heist at play, and I'm the only one that seems to realize it!"

I looked over at Adina, who was holding her microphone up to capture Zach's spur-of-the-moment drama in all its glory. She was lapping up Zach's performance, and I could tell this would be gold for her podcast, even if it did amount to nothing.

"Okay, run it by me then," I said. "What's going on at the museum?"

Zach pointed up to the glass display cabinet on the wall, the same one housing the four tools of Anubis. "No one else seems to realize it, and they don't believe me anyway. Someone swapped out one of the artifacts."

"Which one?" Adina asked.

"The scepter, Anubis' most powerful tool!" Zach said in dismay.

"What makes you so sure of this?" I asked.

Zach pressed his lips together and moved his head from side to side. "I… I don't know. It's just this feeling. Like I *know* that the scepter has been swapped around. Now don't get me wrong the thing up there in that display is a convincing forgery, but it's not the real one, it's not the one that arrived when the exhibit came to the museum last year."

I walked towards the wall to get a closer look at the glass cabinet and stared at the artifacts. From where I was standing, they all looked real, and from the sounds of things Zach's suspicions were dubious at best—he was going off intuition, there was no real evidence to display.

It was then that I noticed I was perhaps being a little hypocritical, more often than not my magic deduction operated on powers of intuition, so it was a little unfair to discredit Zach just because he was following his gut. That's when I noticed something else, the slightest crackling sensation on my fingertips, as though there was electricity in the air.

Magic!

I blinked my eyes in the deliberate manner that activated my witch sight, and then I saw something truly astonishing. Around three of the four artifacts, faint lines of purple magic moved and crackled through the air, invisible to the other mortals standing around me. The scepter, the same one that Zach accused as being fake, had no such lines—it was definitely different from the rest. I blinked again to deactivate my witch sight and looked back at Zach and Adina.

"You're right, the scepter has been swapped out. It's a fake."

Adina's face lit up in amazement. "How could you possibly know that?!"

"Just call it a hunch," I said. "I bet my bottom dollar though, if they tested that scepter up there it would come back as fake." I looked at Zach. "Hasn't anyone done that?"

"They're not interested!" he said in dismay. "The museum head is usually great for that sort of thing, but it's like she's under some spell or something, it's like everyone is! They're all just so... ignorant—for lack of a better world."

"Your colleagues are acting strangely?" I asked.

"Only concerning this. For everything else they're normal, but whenever I bring up this I get laughed out of the building."

"Hm." I crossed my arms and paced away from the wall. I had to admit this *did* have my interest now. "Do you have any suspects?" I asked.

"Only one, and I haven't seen them in months. They left right around the time the switch happened, and I haven't seen them since."

"Who was that?" I asked.

"Lyle, the janitor! I've tried to get in contact with him but as far as I know he's left town. He went north back to Babonix. Apparently, that's where he's from originally."

"Babonix?" I said in fascination. The small ski-town on the northern tip of Pendle Island was no stranger to me. It occurred to me at that moment that there was another unanswered mystery lying in wait for me there, a problem I had been neglecting up until now.

"I can see those gears turning, Chelsea," Adina remarked. "What are you thinking?!"

"I'm thinking there might be more here than meets the eye."

Zach's face lit up. "So, you're going to help?"

"I'll do my best. One thing is for sure. Something unusual is going on here. I'll need a photo of this janitor, Zach."

It seemed there was a mystery afoot at the museum after all.

CHAPTER 6

The next morning, I put the museum mystery on the backburner and set my sights on another problem that I had been putting off—The Brewdock Witches on Isle Vassago. With my Cousin Lizzy and Aunt Glenda for backup we hired a small boat and set off from the shores of Pendle Island in the early hours of the morning. The air was cold and crisp, the steely grey waves lapping up against the sides of the boat as we hunkered down tight.

Sailing away from the island and into the endless blue felt a little daunting at first, it was hard to believe there was anything out there at all.

After fifteen minutes though a small shape did appear on the horizon, and as we drew closer it became the elusive Vassago Isle, a small island that couldn't have been more than a mile or two on each side. On the right side of the isle a sheer face of rock jutted up from the horizon, and above that there stood a castle that seemed impossibly large, its towers, buttresses and columns forking up towards the stormy heavens. We were all wrapped in large raincoats, a sprinkle of cold drizzle pattering down upon us.

"Cream on a cracker," Glenda remarked. "That thing looks like it came straight out of Dracula."

"That it does," I agreed.

Soon after that the boat pulled up an old jetty. The captain—an ancient fisherman named Abe—tied the boat up and helped us onto the boardwalk. "I've got to head back in an hour," he said, pulling a pipe from his anorak and lighting it up. "If you're not back by then I'll pick you up later."

"Later when?" Lizzy asked.

"Ooh… let's see," Old Abe said as he struggled with his pipe. "By the time I finished with the fishing, probably eight tonight."

The three of us looked at the mist-shrouded island ahead of us and gulped at the prospect of spending an entire day here. "We'll see you in an hour," I said, and then we started walking along the jetty. "Can you signal before you leave?"

"I'll sound the foghorn. When you hear that you have five minutes."

As we walked the old wooden boards creaked underfoot, as though they were going to snap at any moment and send us sinking into the icy cold waters below. Through the curling wall of fog ahead I could see the vague shapes of buildings and towering above us on the right was the unescapable silhouette of the cold, dark castle.

"Anyone else getting real bad vibes from this place?" Lizzy said warily. The three of us were uncharacteristically quiet, and as we walked away from the dock the sound of the crashing waves was really the only sound around us.

"Eh, it's not so bad," Glenda said. "I've been here once; it was like this last time."

"What's here?" I asked her.

"There's a little one street town. A permanent fishing settlement, though I don't think many people live here now. Then there's the castle of course, but there's no missing that thing."

We walked through the fog, and it started to clear a little. As it did, I saw an old weatherworn sign, one half had fallen to the ground, and it was tilted.

Welcome to Humdrum. Population: 30.

"Talk about a small town," Lizzy said under her breath.

Walking a little further the fog started to roll back, revealing a small one-street town of old wooden houses that looked swollen from decades of seawater. We rounded the corner onto the street, and I realized the building we were standing next to was a general store, a faded sign hanging over its main window that said, 'Hop's Shop.' Inside it looked dark and dusty.

"Okay so it wasn't this creepy last time," Glenda said, the three of us standing with our breath held as we stared out at the ghost town. The light drizzle of rain momentarily receded as the fog continued to retreat, revealing the town in all its ghostly splendor. It really was like something out of a horror movie.

"We all done then?" Lizzy said. "Let's get back on that boat and go home!"

"Not so fast," I said. "We have to find these Brewdock witches once and for all and confront them, we need to find out what's going on here. Has everyone else forgot they tried to take over the island this month?"

"No," Lizzy grumbled.

"Stupid Brewdocks," Glenda joined in.

It looked like there was another community-type building at the end of the street, a bar and an inn maybe. As we were by the store it made sense to check it out now. "Come on," I said. "Let's see if anyone can help us out in here."

I walked up to the front door of the general store and tried to open it. It was locked. "That's a sign," Lizzy said. "We should leave!" I gave my cousin a disapproving look and turned back to the locked door.

"Weird, the opening hours say it should be open now," I said, looking at the times printed on the inside of the door's glass window.

"Chelsea darling, it doesn't look like anything in this town has been open for the better part of three decades. Maybe we *should* skedaddle?" Glenda suggested.

"No," I said, shaking my head. "There has to be someone here we can talk to." I looked back at the looming figure of the castle overhead. It was hard to tell, but there had to be some sort of path up to that place, hidden in the tall rockface upon which the castle stood.

"There!" Lizzy shrieked, her panic making the three of us jump. One of her hands slapped on my shoulder, and the other pointed down the street. "There's someone down there!"

The three of us looked down the street to the distant inn, and sure enough we saw a head sticking out of a door, staring back at us. As soon as Lizzy reacted the distant figure disappeared back inside the building and slammed the door shut.

"I think I'm going to vomit out of fear," Glenda croaked.

"You and me both," Lizzy said.

"Look it's probably a misunderstanding. Let's just go and talk to that person and figure out what the heck is going on here. I mean… someone has to have an answer. This *isn't* scary." Nope, not one bit. *Keep telling yourself that Chelsea.*

With a silent gulp I clenched my fists and started walking down the street, checking over my shoulder to make sure Glenda and Lizzy were following—they were, though reluctantly and several paces behind me.

Within a minute I reached the old sea-worn inn at the other end of the street. I climbed up onto its wooden porch and rapped my fingers on the door. "Hello? It's Chelsea Sponks! I've come to speak with the Brewdocks! We need to put this feud behind us!"

I heard a thud from somewhere inside the old wooden building. Looking back again I saw Glenda and Lizzy stood on the other side of the street, clinging onto one another. They offered me a thumbs up and a nod of encouragement. *Real helpful guys.*

Another thud followed and then I heard a latch on the other side of the door. It opened very slowly and through the crack I saw a mass of wild black hair and two glassy black eyes. "Sponks, the High Witch."

"That's me, I've come to talk. What's your name?"

"Belladonna," the woman on the other side of the door said. "Belladonna Brewdock."

My blood momentarily went cold at the mention of the name. This was my first time meeting a Brewdock witch, and by all accounts they were dangerous people, not to be trusted.

"Do you know why I'm here?" I asked. I knew full well the Brewdock witches were responsible for the attack on the island last month, but I wanted to see if this woman would be truthful with me.

"I can only draw one logical conclusion," the woman said warily. "You've come to kill me."

The unexpected statement was so extreme it made me do a doubletake. "Hang on, what? No, I haven't come here to kill you."

"Then the only other option is that you've come here to help me."

"What are you talking about?" I asked, wondering why this woman was dealing in these bizarre extremes.

"He's taken everyone else," she said. "I'm the only one left. Still, he's already got to me."

"I'm sorry, but I'm very confused—" I said. "Can you explain what you're talking about?"

"Him," she said, jerking her head in the direction of the castle. "The mad man on the hill. Taking people and… doing his thing to him."

"What thing?" I asked, wondering what on earth this woman was talking about.

That was when she pulled back the door and I saw her body for the first time, though her top half was comparatively normal, her bottom half was completely alien. Instead of legs there was a tangle and mess of—

"Are those tentacles?!" I gasped, stepping back from the door. I half expected this half-woman half-beast to jump at me, but instead she shrank inside the building, leaving the door wide open.

"Come in," she said grimly. "We can talk all about it."

* * *

FOR A MOMENT I waited on the old porch, and I stared into the dark hallway of the wet and dusty house. Looking back over my shoulder once more I saw Lizzie and Glenda still huddled on the other side of the street. I jerked my head in motion for them to come over, but they didn't move at first.

"What are you doing?" I hissed. "I thought you were supposed to be here to back me up. Glenda, you're supposed to be the toughest one on the island." The only reason I brought my eccentric aunt along was because she wasn't afraid of anything. So far, the only thing she and Lizzie had done was cowering about 10 paces behind me and I wasn't sure I could say it was all that helpful.

"Don't take it personally Chelsea," Glenda said, "I've just got the heebie-jeebies and all. The last time I was here on this wretched little island I was only a little girl, and it scared the bejesus out of me then too. I think I'm having a panic attack."

"That settles it," Lizzie said, "If Glenda's terrified then I have every reason to be terrified too, maybe we should just go back to the boat and wait for Chelsea to finish."

"Or..." I said slowly, "You could both get your butts over here before I use my magic to turn you into a couple of toadstools. I don't know if either you just noticed but a half woman half octopus answered the door and I think I could use a little backup here."

My threat seemed to breathe a new lease of life into my unhelpful companions, the pair of them gave each other an unsure look and they quickly crossed the road and ran up the porch steps to stand behind me. I smiled now that they were finally being useful.

"That's more like it! Now let's get inside and listen to what this crazy woman has to say."

"Who is she, a Brewdock?" Lizzie asked.

"Yes. She said her name was belladonna Brewdock she seemed to think that I've come here to kill her or help her."

"Seems a little extreme," Glenda said.

"Yeah, well it seems like we're living in extreme times. Or at least on Vassago Isle we are."

With a big breath to steady myself I clenched my fists and stepped through the old doorway, walking into the dark and dusty hall. The entire building smelled like salt, barnacles, and putrid seaweed. It was bone chillingly cold, and my breath misted on the air.

"Through here!" Belladonna shouted from a room at the back of the building. Meagre light poured from an open door at the other end of the room, through which I could see the makings of a messy kitchen. I walked forward reluctantly into the old kitchen and saw the half squid woman standing at a stove with an old black metal kettle in her hand. Belladonna didn't look back at me, but she seemed to know I was there. "Do you want tea?" she asked.

For a moment I wondered if I should take a drink from this woman, there was the potential that she was my enemy and could use this opportunity to poison me, but my intuition told me she posed no immediate threat.

"Sure, my friends, Lizzie and Glenda, will take a cup too if that's not too much trouble," I said.

This time Belladonna did look over to regard my accomplices lurking behind me in the door, her eyes narrowed in slight interest, and she lifted her head a little and laughed under her breath.

"So, you brought a whole party to lynch me, did you?" she asked.

The question automatically put me on the defensive. "Nothing like that," I said, "You have to appreciate we had no idea what we were walking into when we came here. It was only very recently the island was attacked, and we had no idea what kind of reception was waiting here for us."

Once again Belladonna laughed under her breath. "Well, I bet you weren't expecting this," she said. Belladonna moved away from the stove, her tentacles rolling across the floor as she approached the table and set down a tray with a kettle and several empty cups. "Sit down and we can talk all about it. I don't bite."

I was the first to move forward. The table was round with six chairs around it. I took a seat opposite from Belladonna and looked back to see Lizzy and Glenda still waiting in the doorway. "Are you coming or not?" I asked.

"Of course," Lizzy laughed nervously. She made her way forward, pushing Glenda along with her as she did so. The pair of them sat on either side of me, it looked like the three of us were interviewing Belladonna for a job position. My mind ran away, imagining what types of questions might come up, or even what job she'd be interviewing for. *So how did you get the tentacles? Can you work weekends?*

Belladonna said nothing as she poured the cups of tea. With a gentle flick of her wrist, she sent the three cups sliding across the table to stop in front of us. She picked up her cup and drank, her wild black eyes regarding me all the while.

"So, this is what Sponks witches look like these days," Belladonna remarked and set her cup back down. Lizzy and Glenda hadn't yet touched their cups, so I picked mine up and had a sip to be polite. The tea tasted normal enough, but the air was so salty it impaired the flavor. "Tell me, how are things back on the mainland?"

"Normal enough," I answered. "Well, as normal as things can be over there anyway."

"Hm," was all Belladonna said as she took another sip. "Yes, things have certainly been more interesting since you came here, eh? If the papers are to be believed you've been busy running all over the island causing trouble."

"Causing and fixing," I said in my defense. "But enough about me. Let's cut to the chase. What's going on here? Why did the Brewdock witches attack the island last month, and how do we put this fighting behind us?" I took another sip of the salty tea, my face contorting a little as I did so.

"I don't know what attack you're referring to, but I can assure you it had nothing to do with me or my kin," Belladonna said dismissively.

"And what about Alison Brewdock?" I asked. "She's in prison now, arrested by Magical Crimes Investigation after putting the entirety of Pendle Island under a huge illusion. She turned everyone into teenagers."

Belladonna suddenly took note at mention of Alison's name. She put her cup down onto the table, it rattled, and tea spilled out. "You've seen Alison? Where is she?!"

"She's behind bars," I said. "Wherever witches and wizards go when they commit magical crimes." I paused for a moment upon reflection that I actually didn't realize *where* that was.

Belladonna's wary black eyes were wide and animated. "So, she's alive..." she said under her breath, speaking mostly to herself. A small smile tugged at her lips. "Perhaps there is hope after all."

I shared a silent glance with Lizzy and Glenda—who still hadn't touched their drinks—I didn't know what was going on with Belladonna, but perhaps she was more unhinged than I realized.

"I'm confused, you're saying you didn't know about the attack on the island?" I asked.

Belladonna snapped from whatever daydream she had slipped into and stared at me. "What? No. I have no idea what you're talking about girl. I thought you came here to help, not throw baseless accusations around."

"Isn't Alison part of your coven though?" Lizzy asked, seemingly finding her courage for the first time since arriving on the island. "You would know about her magic activity. A spell of that level required several witches to coordinate it."

"Alison has been missing for three months," Belladonna said simply. "She was amongst the first to go, when he started taking them."

The three of us looked at one another again. I'm not sure what it was, but Belladonna had a natural way of creeping people out. "Who started what now?" I asked. "What are you referring to?"

"Mordoc," she answered. "That slimly little weasel hiding up in the castle."

"Hold up a second," I asked. "Who is Mordoc, and what does he have to do with any of this?"

"He's the one you're after," Belladonna said. "The mad wizard. He took the castle from the Brewdocks, he's taken the people from the island. He's mad, and I suspect he's the one that made Alison perform that magical attack. He's the one that did this to me." Belladonna pushed back from the table and one of the black tentacles lifted up into the air.

I gulped. "You're saying you're not the bad guy here?" I asked.

Belladonna lifted a brow in intrigue and shook her head in disbelief. "Are you finally cottoning on to that?"

"Who is he then?" Lizzy asked. "And what does he want?"

Belladonna's black eyes sparkled with a strange and malignant sadness. "He wants power. He wants the island. He wants... everything."

CHAPTER 7

"*L*et's rewind a little here," I said to Belladonna. "Who is this Mordoc character and how did he do this to you?"

"Let me ask you a question first," Belladonna said. "You came in here with the opinion that Brewdock witches were responsible for the happenings on your island recently. Now how did you get an idea like that in your heads?"

I paused for a moment and looked at my accomplices before answering Belladonna. Up until now I hadn't gotten the sense that she was a threat or danger to us but if there was a chance she took offense at the idea of being made out to be the bad guy then I had to tread carefully. I decided that honesty would be the best policy.

"It's to do with that castle up there on the other end of the isle. It's my understanding that castle belongs to a vampire named Count Vassago. Vassago came to me recently and asked for my help, he said he'd left the island centuries ago and, in his absence, the Brewdock witches, who had been his faithful servants up until then, took the castle from under his feet while he was gone."

Belladonna considered the information for a moment, a blank expression on her weathered face. After a second of measured consideration, she threw back her head and laughed, a shrill cackle erupting from her mouth. "Ha ha ha!" she said heartily. "My my, Count Vassago doesn't change *does* he," she said rhetorically.

"What's that supposed to mean?" Lizzy asked.

"Well, you've heard Vassago's side of things, so it only seems fair that you should now hear mine," Belladonna said. "That old vampire will say anything to make himself look better, I can't say it surprises me, he's always been a vain old bat."

"So, let's hear your side of things then," I said, "What's the truth, is Vassago lying?"

Again, Belladonna chuckled to herself, like she was in on a joke that only she understood. "Just a smidgen. Here's what really went down. The Brewdock witches and Vassago always had a good relationship. He was a powerful vampire, and we were able witches with the ability to help him in whatever magic he was trying to do. My ancestors were the ones that helped him build that castle, and their descendants were the ones that helped him maintain it.

"Every generation of Brewdock witches has lived and died in that castle. After its completion Vassago lived happily at the side of the Brewdock witches, together in the castle for around one hundred years. Did he tell you why he built the castle in the first place?"

"I don't believe so; I'm assuming it has something to do with this demonic power that supposedly lives underneath the castle?" I asked.

Belladonna nodded her head. "You are entirely correct, though there's no supposing about it, a demonic entity *does* live under that castle. Before Vassago and my ancestors built that castle this isle was just a piece of rock with a hole at its northern end. The hole is still there to this day, though now it's hidden in the depths of the castle foundations. It's about twenty feet across and it's essentially a tunnel that stretches down to the magma of the earth, it's within that fiery domain the demon Bahmut resides."

"But what did Vassago strive to achieve by building that castle?" I asked.

"He wanted to take advantage of the demon's power, and he did a little bit, being in the presence of Bahmut made Count Vassago a stronger vampire, and it made us Brewdock witches stronger too, but we soon realized that spending too long in the presence of the demon had an unusual effect on one's mind, it was starting to turn us all mad."

"Mad?" I asked. I stared at Belladonna for a moment as I awaited her answer, it wasn't necessarily difficult to believe that everyone that lived on this bizarre little island was crazy, but I needed her to elaborate a little.

"Yes, positively mad," Belladonna said. "That's part of the reason Vassago left, though he'll never admit it. He realized that building the castle was a mistake, he thought he could control the demon underneath the earth, but it was too strong, even for him. So, the vampire left, he framed his departure as mere boredom, he said he had grown tired of the island and wanted to travel again. In his absence he left us as the caretakers and we've been keeping check of things ever since, taking care of the mess the vampire left behind."

"So, you're saying that Vassago is actually the bad guy in all of this?" Glenda asked.

Belladonna tilted her head from side to side as though weighing up the question. "I think that 'bad guy' doesn't really apply to anyone in this situation apart from Mordoc of course."

I took another sip of my salty tasting tea and put the cup back down on the table. "I intend to ask you about him in a moment, but what I want to know is how did the Brewdock witches contain this demonic power underneath the castle if the vampire Vassago couldn't do it?"

"It's a good question," Belladonna sad. "The simple answer is that we treated it with respect. After Vassago left and it became clear that he wasn't coming back my ancestors took steps to put distance between them and the evil lurking underneath the castle. They permanently closed the lower floors of the castle and left it well alone —that's the best thing to do to keep him happy."

"OK..." I said. "So, what's been going on since then?" I asked. "Who is this Mordoc character and what is he up to?"

"He first appeared around a year ago," Belladonna said, "He said he'd come to the island to conduct some magical experiments. At the time we thought nothing of it, he was pretty quiet and kept to himself, no one really took any notice of him. That all changed when he gained access to the castle," Belladonna explained.

"Was the castle off limits before that?" Glenda asked.

"Oh yes," Belladonna said enthusiastically, "The castle is off limits to anyone that isn't a Brewdock witch, it's always been like that, has been since Vassago built the castle all those centuries ago."

"How many Brewdock witches are there now?" Lizzy asked

"These days?" Belladonna asked. "Well, I have my suspicions that I'm the last one left, Mordoc got to everyone else. There were just under ten of us living on this island before all this nonsense started. My two oldest sisters, Drucilla and Elsbeth, and then my younger sister whom you already seem to know, Allison. Then there was my mother and her two sisters and our grandmother, Elana."

"How did Mordoc access the castle?" I asked Belladonna.

"He's cunning and sly," she explained. "Alison fell for him immediately, he wrapped her right around his finger, I'll tell you that for free. Alison is a sweet girl, don't get me wrong, but she's a fool for love. Mordoc saw that and took advantage of it. How he got inside the castle I don't actually know, but I think it had something to do with Alison."

"And what about… those," Glenda said hesitantly, looking at the writhing tentacles moving about beneath Belladonna's waist.

"Yes, quite grotesque, aren't they?" Belladonna said in agreement, though none of us had actually said as much out loud. "They are a recent change, all thanks to that lunatic holed up there in the castle."

"You're saying this Mordoc character did this to you?" Lizzy asked.

"Yes, that's what he does. There's only a small population on this island, so we noticed pretty quickly when people started disappearing. After Mordoc took control of the castle he kicked the rest of the witches out and we came back down here to the town below. He put magical wards up around the castle, preventing anyone from getting back in. Now the drawbridge is up, and no one's been able to get in since."

"Tell us about the people going missing," I asked.

"Tom Loren was the first," Belladonna recalled. "He's a young fisherman, deals with trout mostly. We noticed he was missing in the evening, went and checked and found his boat on the dock, looked like he hadn't even been out that morning. Then that night we heard the calamity at the castle. Strange screams, thunder striking the high tower, the windows flashing with ghastly light. A few days later we caught sight of him for the first time, it was late at night, I was putting the trash out—I saw this *creature...* half Tom Loren, and the other half... I don't know, maybe a Lion? Lurking in the alleyway. It disappeared before I could get a closer look."

"You think this Mordoc is abducting people and performing magical experiments on them?" Glenda asked.

"I *know* he is, because he did it to me," Belladonna said, slapping one of those tentacles down on the table as a stark reminder. The weight of it made the cups clatter, and we all jumped back in our chairs. "One by one everyone on this island has vanished, taken by that mad man in the castle. He came for me last, dragging me away in my sleep. I woke up strapped to a bed, and then he performed that dark magic he's been practicing. I asked him what the point of this all was, what he wanted to achieve. That's when I saw it—utter madness in his eyes. He must have gone straight down to the depths to see Bahmut himself, the power has driven him mad. None of us ever got close to the demon, not even Vassago or my ancestors, that's a sure-fire way to lose your mind straightaway."

"What does he want, this Mordoc character?" I asked.

"Now? Everything. His mind is gone, and the only thing left is a salacious greed that feeds his insanity. He told me he was building an army, creatures with the strength of beasts, and the cunning of man."

Suddenly my mind flashed back to something I had seen on the island a few months back, a curious creature in the woods that was half-man, half-beast. "I've seen one of these things, on the island!"

"I'm sure you have. Mordoc sends the creatures out to bring back new victims. I tried to get away before he could change me, but I was too late, now I look like...this."

"How did you escape?" Lizzy asked.

"Mordoc is beginning to lose control of himself, his madness is making him sloppy. As soon as he changed me, he unbuckled the restraints and before I knew it, he was gone, I suspect he had ventured back down to the depths to draw more power from the demon well. He's addicted now, he cannot stop himself. Getting out of the castle was easy, I escaped a week ago. In that time, I expected he would send his minions back after me, but none have come. I think he has forgotten about me or is up to something else entirely. Either way this is me now… a lone beast, lost and forgotten, wondering what I can do to stop the madman on the hill."

"Why do men ruin everything?" Glenda asked. Belladonna chuckled lightly at the question, though from the bleak dark of her eyes I could see the weight of her situation was pulling her down.

"So, there you have it," Belladonna recollected, "You're all caught up to speed now. Mordoc is insane and before long he will attack the island again. I have no way inside the castle, and he's too strong for me to contend with now, but possibly *you* can do something about it," she said, looking at me.

"Me, what can I do?" I asked.

"I don't know," Belladonna said with a shrug. "Use that inordinate amount of magic you're sitting on. You're the High Witch, if anyone can do something, it's you."

"But I—" I faltered, wondering exactly why I was hesitant to help this woman. Nothing she had said so far seemed out of place, and I got the impression she was telling me the truth, but still… Vassago had taught me to be cautious, and I thought I could trust *him*.

"You still don't trust me," Belladonna said in realization, her glassy black eyes examining me.

"Don't take it personally," I said, "but up until now I was led to believe the Brewdock witches were my mortal enemies. I mean, Alison *did* try to kill me."

"And me," Lizzy pointed out.

"Under the control of Mordoc," Belladonna said.

"Why didn't he turn her into one of these half-animal beasts?" Lizzy asked.

"Yes, and when Alison was caught, she said she'd attacked the island from the pressure of her family. She said her mother was controlling, overbearing," I said.

Again, Belladonna just laughed and shook her head. "My mother? Elana Brewdock? You'll never meet a gentler woman. No offense, but the Sponks witches have always been the loose cannons on the islands, the Brewdocks were always concerned with keeping things in check, we are quiet groundskeepers, lurking in the background and taking care of things without credit—we want things to keep existing, that's our only interest." She paused and considered me. "You're perhaps the most adjusted Sponks women I've ever met."

"Why would Alison blame her mother though, and Lizzy has a point, why didn't Mordoc turn her into one of these weird animal things?" I asked.

Belladonna shrugged. "I don't know. I know that the animal thing is only half of his power, the other half is taking control of people's minds to make them do his bidding. He did the first part on me, he changed my legs into these darned things, but he let me go before he took control of my mind—like I said, he's getting sloppy. I suspect he didn't change Alison's body because that would diminish her ability to blend in. Alison was always a brilliant witch, Mordoc took advantage of her mind. I suspect the title of High Witch likely would have passed onto her if you hadn't come along."

I listened carefully to Belladonna and took one final sip of the salty tea as I weighed up her words. "I guess I'm just struggling to see who I should believe. There are conflicting stories on both sides, and I'm wary of the Brewdocks after already being double-crossed by Alison —I thought she was my friend."

"I guarantee this, you take down Mordoc and end his magic, and whatever dark hold he has over Alison will break—that girl you made friends with, that wasn't an act, she really is lovely, we all are. Like I said, this ancient feud business is nonsense, it *is* time to put it behind us."

"One thing you haven't explained," I said, "why were you so convinced I was going to kill you when you answered the door?"

"That is usually the custom, when power transfers from one High Witch to another," Belladonna said. "If you're looking for reason to trust me then perhaps this will clear things up." Belladonna then pulled out a small black book from under the table. Its thick leather cover was studded and embossed with golden magical patterns that glowed in the dim room. Lizzy and Glenda both jumped up at once and backed away from the table.

"Alright, easy now!" Glenda said. "Where did you get *that* thing?!"

I watched Belladonna as she placed the book carefully down on the table, visible motes of purple magic crackling in the air around it. I had no idea what this was, but one thing was clear—it was incredibly powerful.

"What's going on here?" I asked, looking back at Glenda and Lizzy, puzzled by their reaction.

"Chelsea, we need to get out of here *now*," Lizzy said. "That's a *Magricon*, an incredibly powerful and dangerous book. She could obliterate everything in a hundred miles of here with one word."

"Very true," Belladonna said casually, "but also a little dramatic. There are thirteen of these books, though most are locked away in secure storage by the MCI. This one here is so powerful that only a High Witch can touch it," Belladonna picked the book up and turned it over in her hands as though it was nothing. "A woman tried to take it from me once—a moment later she was a pile of ash on the floor, just from touching the book."

I gulped and eyed the curious book, more than aware of the strange power beating from it. "You're a High Witch too?" I asked Belladonna.

"I was. My power started fading when you came into your own. Now it's time to pass the buck... quite literally. I hope with this you might find a way to stop Mordoc. It's also customary for the new High Witch to kill the other upon their first meeting."

"Yeah, I'm not going to do that," I clarified.

Belladonna shrugged as if it was no big deal. She put the book down and pushed it across the table. "Traditions are a waste of time anyway. Hopefully this shows you can trust me. Your friend is right, even though my powers are fading, with this book I could have made quick work of you and your friends. We are not enemies though, so that was never my intention, we are allies now—and I'm asking for your help Chelsea Sponks. Take back the castle, stop the mad wizard before it's too late. The book is yours now."

I looked at Glenda and Lizzy, still unsure if I could trust this woman. "Can I touch this thing?"

"Yes," Lizzy said, "but for heaven's sake make sure you put it somewhere safe, and don't let anyone else touch it!"

I stared at the book a moment longer before taking a large breath and reaching out to grab it. I didn't turn into a pile of ash, but I did feel it's strong magical presence crackle and arc against my touch. I slipped the book into my satchel and made sure it was properly closed.

"There you have it," Belladonna said, "centuries of fighting over. We're all friends now. Good luck with Mordoc, you'll need it."

"What are you going to do?" I asked. "You can't sit around waiting here for him to come back for you. Come back to the island with us, we'll make sure you're safe."

"No," Belladonna said and shook her head. "This is my home; I will not leave. It is not in a Brewdock witch's way to flee. I will stay and fight, no matter what the outcome." In the distance I heard the faint wail of the foghorn—a sign that it was time for us to leave. Belladonna noticed the sound and stood up from the table. "It seems it is time for you to leave. I hope to see you back soon, until next time Miss Sponks."

With that the three of us left Belladonna's shack and made our way back to the boat. As we walked back to the jetty, I looked up at the castle looming over our left shoulders and for a moment I could swear I saw a figure watching me from one of its windows.

Come visit Chelsea, a voice said in my mind. *You'd make a great addition to the team.*

CHAPTER 8

*A*fter getting back to the island I said goodbye to Glenda and Lizzy, making sure to add a sarcastic thanks for them having my back. Once back at my house I found Adina in the kitchen, she was drinking a cup of coffee by herself at the kitchen table while holding her microphone in her other hand.

"Ceilings—they're unusual things. They're always there, looking down on us, hearing our every secret, but how often do we look back and wonder if anyone is listening? A hidden camera, a secret microphone, one has to stop and wonder every now and then if—"

"Still recording?" I asked as I walked into the kitchen.

"You betcha!" Adina said, hitting stop on her recorder and putting down her mic. "Oh man I'm pumped and ready to get out there for another day of discovery. How was your morning of errands?"

When I'd left that morning, I hadn't told Adina where I was going or what I was up to—I couldn't really, it was witch business, and I couldn't share that sort of thing with mortals. I'd just told her that I had some errands and appointments that I had to attend do —privately.

"My morning was *revealing*, certainly not what I was expecting," I said. I couldn't say more on the matter to Adina, but my answer had been truthful even if vague. My meeting with Belladonna *had* been completely unexpected, and if I was going to believe her side of things—which I actually was starting to do—the Brewdocks weren't my enemy at all, this mysterious Mordoc was to blame.

"Well, I know that look. Say no more, I can tell when someone doesn't want to spill a secret," Adina said, finishing the last of her coffee. "Are you ready to go and meet with Dec? I barely slept last night I was so excited over the prospect of getting to talk to him one-on-one!"

"We both have very different definitions of what we find exciting," I chuckled under my breath, "but yes, I'm ready to hit the road, do you want to grab a bite to eat on the—"

My phone cut my question short, I pulled it out and answered it. From the screen I could see it was Dec.

"Change of plan," he said in answer.

"You're cancelling the meeting?" I asked.

"What? No! That would be crazy. You're my holy grail, I need you! I just don't want to meet at the golf club is all, seems like a waste of time. I've got a better place in mind."

"Bowling? Ice hockey?" I joked.

"My old house, where the crime took place. I still own it, though I haven't been there since everything happened. I figured it would be a good use of time to take you there, show you the scene directly, let you work your magic. You can't do much sleuthing on a golf course."

"You'd be surprised," I said, "but sure, let's meet at the house instead. Can you send me the details?"

"Already have," Dec King grunted. "See you there in fifteen minutes." Without another word the hardware magnate ended the call. I put my phone back in my pocket and looked at Adina. "Your morning just got better, King wants to meet at his old house, not the golf course."

"Wait a second, you mean we actually get to go to the scene of the crime?!" Adina said, her voice so high-pitched with excitement it could wake dogs.

"I knew you'd be up for it. Listen, can you do me a favor, I just need to make a personal call really quick. Do you want to wait for me in the van and I'll be out in a few minutes? Sorry to delay, but it's quite important."

"Sure," Adina said. "It'll give me a chance to listen over the footage I was recording when you came in."

"Right, the ceiling commentary. More B-sides?"

"Low level stuff like that is better suited for my C-sides. I put them as secondary episodes every week, people still seem to love them though. Someone once told me I have a very hypnotic voice."

"I can see that," I said. Adina did have this odd quality to her voice, smooth and crackly, like an old vinyl recording flowing through the air.

Adina skipped out of the kitchen and out the front door. I double checked to make sure she was gone and then I called Artemis. "Hey! Come out! She's gone!" A second later a patter of pawprints came down the stairs. Artemis yawned and sat down in front of me.

"Oh man, I was starting to think she was *never* going to leave. Do you know how exhausting it is not being able to talk in your own house?"

"There's a first time for everything," I said. "Listen, I've got something super important that I have to talk to you about, and not a lot of time to do so, so I need you to be helpful, okay?"

"Alright, lay it on me," Artemis said. "What's going on?"

I opened up my satchel and pulled out the small black book that Belladonna had given me. The Magricon crackled with strong purple magic, it felt like a magnet in my hands. Artemis' eyes opened wide, and he jumped onto his feet, his haunches raised.

"Meow! Where the heck did you get that thing?!" he said, jumping back from me.

"You know what it is?" I asked.

"Of course, I know what it is! It's a Magricon. It's the magical equivalent of a nuclear bomb! Why do you have it?!"

"Belladonna Brewdock gave it to me, she said only a High Witch can hold it."

"She was a High Witch? Huh. I didn't know that. Well okay, yeah, this is pretty serious. What do you want to do with this thing?"

"I don't know, but I don't want to be carrying it around in a satchel all day. Is there anywhere safe I can store this thing? Somewhere in the house that I can lock it away?"

Artemis thought for a moment and then nodded his head. "There's Griselda's old safe in the basement."

"There isn't a safe in the basement," I remarked.

Artemis cackled. "Oh sweet, naïve, Chelsea. You think you know all the secrets of this house because you've lived here for a year? Follow me."

I followed Artemis into the kitchen and down the stairs that led to the basement. I pulled the string that turned on the weak yellow bulb and regarded the dingy basement that sat underneath the house. There was an old boiler in one corner, a spare bed in the other, and in between those corners there were endless heaps of old junk that needed throwing out. This place could probably make a nice game room if it had a little makeover.

"So, I see a mountain of junk, but no safe," I said.

"Oh, ye of little faith," Artemis tutted as he weaved through the piles of junk. "Follow me." The little black cat led me across the basement to an old piano and he jumped up on the stool. "So, I've tried to do this, but never could—you know, paws and all. Can you play me chopsticks?"

"Chopsticks, seriously?" I asked. "Stop messing around, I thought you were showing me this safe."

"I am, Griselda hid it behind a magical charm in this piano. Just play the darn tune."

I approached the piano, positioned my fingers over the black keys and played the brief piece that every child, teenager, and adult plays at least once in their life. A second later the basement started to rumble, the piano slid back into the wall and a metallic safe door appeared, like a lost object rising from the depths of a forgotten lake.

"This isn't a safe, it's a vault!" I said in surprise. I was now standing in front of a huge metal door with a heavy-looking spoked handle in its center, a combination lock just off to the side. "But what's the—"

"Cat, Bat, Pumpkin, Pumpkin, Broom, Hat, Boots," Artemis said.

"What?"

"That's the combination. Look at the tumbler. It's symbols not numbers. There are seven dials, and each dial has like twenty different pictures on it. Griselda designed it herself, she was eccentric you know."

"Yeah, I'm starting to pick up on that. Tell me the combination again?" Artemis rattled off the combination again and as I turned the last dial to 'Boots' I heard a click in the door. I turned the giant spoked handle anti-clockwise, and the vault popped open with a giant *thud*. I pulled open the door and saw a room inside, lined with shelves containing all sorts of intriguing items. Magical books, curious looking objects, a jewelry box, old folders with paperwork inside.

"I can't believe you never told me about this place," I said.

Artemis shrugged. "You never asked. Besides, it's just a bunch of dumb old junk. It's not like there's food hidden down here or anything."

I took the Magricon out of my bag, wrapped it in an old cloth from one of the shelves and stashed it behind a box of old photographs. A moment later it was sealed shut in the vault. The door disappeared and the piano slid forward from the wall again. I let out a breath of relief. "That's a weight off my shoulders. Just don't go messing around in there, and don't tell anyone else about it," I said to Artemis.

"Um reminder, these paws can't play chopsticks, and I'm not allowed to tell anyone else about it, it's one of those familiar oaths. Even *I* can't break them."

"Good, well I'm going out with Adina again, we've got stuff to do. Will you look after the house?"

"I've managed a couple of centuries so far, I'm sure I can manage another afternoon," Artemis said sarcastically.

"Atta kitty." I gave him an approving scritch behind the ears and sprinted back up the basement steps to meet Adina outside. We had a meeting with a crime scene, and I didn't want to be late.

* * *

NOT LONG AFTER that Adina and I pulled up outside the gated house belonging to Declan King. As we did so the gates opened, and I saw Dec climb out of a fancy-looking Mercedes that was parked on the drive. Adina and I both climbed out of the van and walked over to meet him.

"Am I glad to see you," Dec said. "Finally, this nightmare can be over." Dec paused and looked at Adina and her unusually decorated van. "What is this?"

"I'm Adina, Adina Lopez, I host a true crime podcast. We're covering this case, do you mind being recorded?"

"Not at all," Dec said with little consideration. "The more people that hear about this the better. I'm innocent, I tell you, innocent! Ever since Meredith died there's been a stigma attached to my name. My business is going down the drain, I need to clear the waters! Where do we start?"

"Well, I—" I paused, looking at the scene around me. Dec's old house was a large two-story building, white plaster walls, clay roof tiles and an arched terrace that ran across the front. Tall mangrove trees surrounded the property, and tall white walls bordered the property completely, sealing it off from the outside. "Tall walls," I remarked. "What are they? Twelve, fifteen feet?"

"Fifteen," he said. "The estate agent said the property is a mission revival gem, though I don't know what that means. I always felt like it was a fortress, until—well, you know."

"So, the morning Meredith died, where were you?" I asked, turning my attention back on Dec. From the pictures and footage, I'd seen of him he seemed like a big man, but in reality, he was actually a little smaller, probably a few inches shorter than myself.

"I was at my apartment in town, Meredith and I had a fight the night before, and we needed a little space from each other."

I raised a querying brow. "Oh?"

"Look I know what you're going to say, don't you think I've already heard all this a hundred times before? Meredith and I had a fight the night before she died, I went to stay at the apartment—of which there is no proof—and the next morning she turns up dead. Very convenient! I know how it looks!"

"Why is there no proof you stayed at the apartment?" I asked.

Dec opened his mouth to answer but Adina got there first. "The surveillance cameras were playing up at the time. No one has ever been able to substantiate Declan King's alibi." Adina laughed nervously as Dec stared at her.

"It seems like *she's* familiar with the case."

"True crime fan!" Adina said, raising a hand as though in confession. "This case is one of my favorites!"

"Yeah well, I want to turn it into ancient history. What do you think Miss Sponks?" Dec asked me.

"I think I need to know more first," I said. "Let's take a look around."

First of all, we lapped the house. Because of the specific architecture style most of the windows were iron-lattice glass. The doors were solid-oak, heavy, and impossible to kick in. At the back of the property there was a large glass patio door. "The patio window was broken," Dec said as we reached the back. "But from the glass on the floor it looked like it was broken from the inside, so there must have been another entry point."

"When they found Meredith all the windows and doors were locked," Adina recalled.

"What other point of entry is there?" I asked.

"The garage," Declan answered. "We had a clicker for it. I had one, and Meredith had one too, though hers was damaged. We were getting it repaired. That's why the police were so convinced I had something to do with it. I was the only person that could access the house, and they could never substantiate my alibi. They said I broke the window to make it look like a burglary gone-wrong."

"Interesting," I said as I contemplated the facts. We went inside the house to see the spot where Meredith had been found, Dec chose to wait outside. While inside Adina was narrating to herself. My eyes moved across the room, looking for any clue or hint that might unravel this mystery. Unfortunately, being here a few years later meant that I'd almost certainly missed any key evidence, most likely the scene had long been disturbed, hiding whatever truths lay in waiting.

"What do you think?" Adina asked me after hitting pause on her recorder.

"Woman dies in her house… its basically physically impossible to get inside other than the garage door, and only the husband has the ability to open it. Whoever killed Meredith broke the window at the back of the house and they did a bad job of it. I gotta say Adina…" I trailed off, looking at her in a certain way to indicate what I thought, but I left it unsaid.

"Everything okay in there?" Dec called.

"Coming back now!" I answered.

Adina and I met Dec in the hall again, he was shifting from foot to foot and looked worn out. "So, what do you think?"

"Were there any other suspects than you?"

Dec shook his head. "No, the police went for me straightaway, they really had it in for me. What do you think? Have you uncovered anything unusual?"

"Not yet," I said. "So far it seems like a mystery. You were the only one with access to the house, I have to admit Mr. King… things don't look good for you."

Dec sighed and rubbed his hands over his face. "Surely there must be something you can do!?"

"Maybe but looking around this house isn't going to give me many answers. Tell you what my fiancé is with Pendle police, maybe I can talk to him and see what he remembers about the case. It might be worth going over the case notes from the time and seeing if anything was overlooked."

"That would honestly be great," Dec said, "I'd appreciate—sorry, wait a second." Dec pulled out his ringing phone and rolled his eyes.

"This place again, sorry I have to take this. The White Flamingo, they won't get off my back."

Dec took the call and walked outside the house. Adina and I listened quietly, the pair of us eavesdropping the call as best we can. It seemed like the call was about money, or a lack thereof. Dec came back a minute later, looking flustered and worn out.

"Business call?" I asked.

"Pleasure, and too much of it. Just some fancy bar my wife, Jennifer, likes to spend her time at. She's built up quite the tab and now I've got to settle the bill. Where were we?"

"I'm going to get a hold of the original case files and see if anything is missing between the lines. After I've had a look at that I'll get back to you with my thoughts, right now… there's not enough to go on."

Dec gave a disappointed sigh and nodded his head. "Very well then. Come on, I'll show you out."

A few minutes later Adina and I were back on the road again, driving away from Dec King's clay-tiled mansion. "Okay, now we're alone you can really tell me what you're thinking," Adina said, hitting the button on her recorder once again.

I watched the tall mangrove trees pass us by as we drove back to the town, my mind trying to figure out an answer that meant Dec King hadn't killed his wife.

"Right now, I can only draw one logical conclusion, Adina," I said.

"What's that?" she asked.

"Dec King killed his wife."

CHAPTER 9

"**W**hat is this place?" Adina asked as we pulled up at the disheveled-looking wooden house on the outskirts of town.

"This is the address of one Lyle Gainsmore, the former janitor of Pendle Museum," I explained. I'd given Adina the address on the way over here, but she was so busy narrating as she drove, she didn't question where we were going.

"Oh, we're doing the museum thing?!" she gasped.

"We are, I need to take a break from Dec King and his business—my mind isn't drawing up any conclusions at the moment. This is kind of how I work best, I get stuck with one thing and focus on something else. Usually when I'm working on that, the answer for the first thing comes to my mind."

"A glimpse inside the mind of an amateur sleuth," Adina said, holding her microphone up to her mouth. "In a lot of ways Chelsea is standing front and center, spinning plates as she runs around, diverting her attention in various directions. When one plate begins to wobble the stage lights gleam off the ceramic, giving her a moment of inspiration for her next problem."

I laughed at the amusing description. "Certainly, one of your more colorful pieces of prose. You strike me as a frustrated writer, have you never thought to write a book?"

"Oh, I've written sixteen," Adina said. "Four already published. Crime novels, obviously. My publisher says I'm a workaholic."

"I am inclined to agree," I said as we exited the van and walked up the path to Lyle's front door. I knocked and waited for a minute—there was no answer.

"I thought that boy back at the museum said that Lyle had left town?" Adina asked.

"He did, but I wanted to check out Lyle's former address first. I thought we might find something worthwhile, potential hints at why a janitor would steal an ancient Egyptian scepter and leave town with it."

"But it's locked, we can't get in there—unless you're suggesting we break in!" she gasped.

"Welcome to the dark side of being an amateur sleuth. You're welcome to leave this part out of your podcast if you want."

"Are you crazy? Why would I leave out gold? How do we get in? Break through the window, climb down the chimney?" Adina was positively buzzing with excitement. If I didn't know any better, I'd say she'd never broken the law in her life.

"I'm uh—" I paused, realizing I couldn't use my magic to break in, not in front of Adina anyway. Or could I? "I'm thinking we go the old-fashioned route. Pick the lock." I pulled a hairpin out of my hair and slid it into the lock. Truth told I had no idea how to pick locks, but it gave me an excuse to obscure the lock while I magically opened it with my other hand.

While I moved the hairpin aimlessly around the lock, I placed my other hand on the handle and willed the lock to open with a burst of magic. Sure enough the tumbler clicked, and I pushed the handle down.

"Okay, I am impressed!" Adina said. "Sleuth and a lock-picking spy, are there any ends to Chelsea Sponks' talents?"

"I'm terrible at ice-skating," I admitted. "Come on, let's hurry inside before anyone sees us."

. . .

LYLE GAINSMORE'S HOME WAS—FOR lack of a better word—a tip, there were stacks of old newspapers piled up by the front door, old take-away containers strewn across every surface, and bags of trash across the floor.

"Looks like old Lyle is something of a hoarder," I said as we moved further into the house. There wasn't much to it, a hallway, kitchen and lounge, with stairs leading up to bedrooms and a bathroom. The whole house was cluttered with trash, and amongst that trash were various sculptures, all of which appeared to be made by Lyle.

"If I didn't know any better, I'd say that Lyle Gainsmore worked in the movie industry," Adina said into her recorder as she walked. "Amongst the piles of trash there are props of one kind or another, everywhere we look. Monster busts, fantastical looking weapons, and it seems that the kitchen is Lyle's main creative base of operations, his artist workshop."

The kitchen was the magnetic center of the house's chaotic mess. Paint-covered newspaper sheets were lain across the kitchen floor, and every counter and surface was full to the brim with old paint cans, brushes, or packets of modelling material.

"I think we just found out how Lyle swapped out the scepter," I said, tapping Adina on the shoulder and pointing at the wall opposite his kitchen table. The wall was full of photographic printouts of the Egyptian artifacts from the exhibit, all photographed from various angles and in close up detail. On the kitchen table there was even an empty mold that matched the outline of the scepter.

"Look at this," Adina said, pulling a framed diploma out from a pile of trash on the kitchen countertop. "Looks like Lyle graduated in sculpture and prop design."

"So, Lyle made a double of the scepter, swapped it for the real one and then left town for Babonix, but why?"

"Maybe he sold the scepter!" Adina suggested. "I bet he could get a pretty penny for that."

"Possibly, Babonix is only a thirty-minute drive from here though, and it's an affluent little skiing town. I don't think there are that many places to fence stolen Egyptian artifacts. There is one thing that has been bothering me, I feel like I recognize this Lyle guy from somewhere."

I pulled out the photo of Lyle, the one that Zach had given me back at the museum. He was a normal enough looking guy, late-thirties, balding with short grey hair and an unassuming face. To be honest the guy didn't have any standout features, he could blend in anywhere, still I'd seen that face somewhere before.

"I could put it on my fan forum, see if one of my Ghoulies can trace him?" Adina suggested.

"What's a *'Ghoulie'*?" I asked, passing her the photo.

"That's what my fans call themselves. They're pretty obsessed."

"Yeah… eh, what the heck. Put it on the forum and see what comes back. Sometimes a fresh set of eyes on things can help give a new perspective." I wandered around the kitchen, staring at the various props Lyle had all over the place. There was no denying it, the guy was talented. I turned back to look at Adina. "So, how long will it take to—"

"Okay got it," Adina said, her phone in her hands. "Someone's replied with a photo of a leaflet from some new-age church, apparently it's on Pendle Island too!"

"Hold on a second, you're telling me you got an answer that fast?" I walked around to look at Adina's phone. She'd made a thread on her forum titled *'Yo Ghoulies, Adina here. Who's this guy?'* and within three minutes she'd had sixty replies. "What the heck!" I said in astonishment.

"Never underestimate the power of a rabid fan base," Adina laughed. "Is this where you recognize the guy?"

"Yes!" I said, looking at the photo of the leaflet one of Adina's fans had replied with. I'd held a similar leaflet myself not long ago after visiting Babonix. "Deacon's ex-girlfriend and father wanted us to check out this new-age church that had just started there. Some guru called Atari Nissan or something like that."

"*Asan Nivon,*" Adina corrected, "and his 'church' is called 'The Temple of the Golden Flute' sounds like a cult alright if you ask me."

"Huh, I've actually been meaning to check out this problem for a while, pretty convenient if it's connected to this stolen Egyptian artifact. I can take out two birds with one stone." I stared at the picture of the guru on the leaflet. There was no denying it, 'Asan Nivon' was Lyle Gainsmore, but he'd grown out a scraggly brown beard, and he had swapped his boiler suit for a red cloak.

"So, Lyle steals an ancient Egyptian scepter, moves to a new town and starts a cult," Adina surmised. "I'll be darned if this island isn't just jam-packed full of exciting oddities! What do you think he's up to up there?"

"I don't know, but I think we should hop in the van, head up there and find out. Let's speak to Lyle himself and see what he has to say."

Adina squeaked with excitement. "This is going to be the best podcast episode, ever! Are you going to listen to it?" she asked me.

"I don't really like the sound of my own voice, but I could make an exception I guess."

"Yes! Let's hit the road! We've got a cult to bust!"

Adina and I left the house and headed back to her skull-adorned podcasting van. The last few weeks had definitely been quiet, but it seemed like the island was more than making up for it now.

* * *

"Tapa gurta!" a robed woman said as Adina and I stepped into the church foyer. It was a small and simple room, with a giant picture of Lyle in his robes on the wall behind the counter. There were plants in the corners and a small fountain bubbling away on the table behind us. "That means 'Warm Welcome' in Sanskrit!"

"How lovely," I said sarcastically, having already heard some of the cult's unusual language choices when I was last in Babonix. "Is Asan around, we need to speak to him," I said.

The robed woman offered us an unusual smile. "Asan's door is always open, but he may be preoccupied at this current moment. If you wait here, I will see if he is taking visitors. My name is Star Flower, by the way."

"Sure it is," I said, watching as 'Star Flower' disappeared through a set of doors. I don't know how Lyle had got his followers to build the church, or even how he'd gotten followers in the first place. The temple looked like it had been thrown up overnight, an unusually shaped building that looked like a cross between a fast-food joint, a monastery, and an alien spaceship. The windows were all triangle shaped, and there wasn't a right angle in sight—all the rooms were circular.

"The Temple of the Golden Flute is an odd place," Adina said into her recorder. "There's a strange energy in the air, and it makes me wonder if there's a cupboard full of Kool-Aid somewhere around the corner..."

"Little chilling, don't you think?" I said as Adina hit pause again.

"Yeah, I'll probably cut that bit out, cults are no joke though. I've done episodes on several different cults, and they rarely end well."

"Good thing you're here, otherwise I'd sign up," I joked.

Just then 'Star Flower' came back through the double doors, smiling at us in her odd and gracious way. "You're in luck. Asan Nivon said the universe instructed him to take in two new disciples today. This might be the beginning of something beautiful. Please, follow me into the temple."

We followed Star Flower through the wooden double doors into the main temple room, a huge circular space filled with cushions and a small stage in the middle. At the very back of the room a huge statue of Lyle—or 'Asan' as he was known to the people here—towered from floor to ceiling, his large eyes staring down at us. In one hand was the scepter, and in the other there was a flute. Currently there weren't many other people around, the few other followers in the temple at the moment were all wearing robes, and they were in silent or group prayer.

"Asan's court is just up here," Star Flower said. We followed her up a set of stairs at the room's edge, a small corridor ended at a set of golden doors. Star Flower paused and knocked. "Sir, the new recruits are here."

"Send them in!" a lofty voice came from the other side. The double golden doors opened on their own, Star Flower bowed to the floor and gestured with one hand for us to go through. "He will see you now," she said in a low and dignified voice.

Adina and I gave each other a momentary glance before heading through the doors. They led into an extravagant looking apartment, a room decorated with gold tapestries, silk throws, every inch of the spacious room filled with plush-looking sofas, futons, or ornate wooden tables.

Incense floated through the air, a serpent-shaped line of grey smoke that wafted across the room. Quiet sitar music seemed to be playing from somewhere.

"I've been expecting you, *Chelsea Sponks*," a disembodied voice said from somewhere within the room. I looked around, wondering where Lyle was exactly, but I couldn't see any sight of him. "It was only a matter of time until you came. You will be my greatest recruit to date —I saw a vision that predicted it."

"Is that so?" I asked. "Listen, we just wanted to talk, Lyle. It's about the scepter you stole from Pendle Museum—we know you swapped it for a fake, one that you made yourself. A pretty convincing job by the way—you should have stuck to the movie industry."

Lyle answered with laughter, like some sort of villain in an action movie. "Please, my name is *Asan Nivon* now, that old name, that belonged to someone else, a person who is dead." Lyle appeared then from a door at the far end of the apartment. He was completely naked, just wrapping himself in a golden gown as he emerged. The scepter was in his hand.

"For the love of—" I said, shielding my eyes from the unwarranted nudity. "You couldn't have put that on before you entered the room?"

"The human body is the greatest gift bestowed upon us from God. We should not be ashamed of it. Here at the Temple of the Golden Flute we embrace our image, we do not shy away from it. You will both learn this when you join our ranks."

Lyle walked forward slowly, like a cat prowling through its territory. He clicked his fingers and a girl suddenly appeared from a side door, a glass of red wine on a silver tray. Lyle took the wine and sipped it as he continued to walk. He sat down on a golden recliner and crossed his legs.

"And what makes you so certain we're going to join this weird little cult?" I asked.

"Everyone that's ever walked through that door has joined," Lyle answered. "They come to learn very quickly that the voice of Asan Nivon can be *very* persuasive, I am the chosen messiah of the new dawn of course, the shepherd who shall lead the flocks to elevated spiritual enlightenment."

For a second neither of us responded, but then Adina did. She pulled out her microphone. "Mental illness comes in many shapes and sizes, be it illusions of grandeur or—"

"That's enough," Lyle said. As he did so I felt the air pulse with the unmistakable hum of magic. Sure enough Adina silenced immediately —something she didn't do often. I activated my witch sight and saw the bright lines of magic throbbing around the scepter in Lyle's hand. That about settled it then, this device was helping Lyle to control people—Zach had said back at the museum that the scepter supposedly did that.

"Not long ago you were a janitor at Pendle Museum, and a hobbyist prop designer too. After leaving the museum—and taking the scepter—you moved up here and set up this cult of yours, care to tell us what's going on, Lyle?"

"I already told you that 'Lyle' is dead," Lyle said. His voice and cadence were still calm, but there was a momentary flash of irritancy in his eyes. Obviously, he wanted to maintain the cool demeanor of an all-knowing leader, but I could see the fragility under the surface. "In that time I have been reborn as Asan Nivon, a messiah that will shepherd humanity into a new age, and—"

"Yeah, yeah," I said, walking forward and picking up one of the unusual golden trinkets that littered the various surfaces of the room. I turned it over and put it back down again. "We've already heard that one. I'm just trying to figure out *why* you're doing this. What's the whole Golden Flute about? How did you come up with all this?"

Lyle blinked at me placidly. I could still feel his subdued anger, but he let out a deep breath and smiled. "The Golden Flute, as you will learn with time, was given to me by god. It lets me play the music that speaks to the soul. Let me illustrate." Lyle moved the flute to his lips and played a short—and unimpressive—ditty, one that sounded faintly middle eastern in origin. He put the flute down again and spoke. "Sit," he ordered.

As he said the word my witch eyes saw the scepter glow with the bright purple light of magic. An invisible pulse of energy swept through the air and Adina sat down at once. I felt the magic pass over me, a warm wall of light that did feel strangely inviting. My legs moved slightly against my own will, but I didn't feel compelled to follow the order.

Asan stared at me with curiosity. "I said, *sit!*" he barked, fear evident in his voice. This time another tide of magic swept through the air. Again, I didn't feel compelled to follow it, but I decided to pretend. I sat down and let mock surprise come over my face. "My goodness! You made me sit!"

"Yes…" Asan said slowly, his fear dissipating slightly as he thought I was under his control. "Now you see the power of the Golden Flute. I play the song of the gods, and mortals respond to my control."

"Amazing!" Adina said, wholly entranced. She wasn't a witch and was therefore more susceptible to magic effects than I was. She had fallen for the magic hook, line, and sinker.

"Yes," I mirrored, pretending to be under the effects of the spell just like Adina. "Truly amazing. Wow Asan, you're so handsome and powerful. We'd love to worship you until the end of our days," I said in my best monotone performance.

Asan rose out of his chair, a dark smile etched across his features. He seemed delighted to have two more humans under the control of his scepter. "You're both going to like it here, you see the Temple is a spiritual initiative, we preach free love here. There are no obligations, but most of our female recruits feel inclined to make love to me."

"Is that so," I said, trying not to throw up in my mouth. "And what is the end goal? World domination? Build a spaceship and fly up to a passing comet? I'm guessing there are limits to that scepter of yours, otherwise you would have brainwashed a lot more people by now."

Lyle stopped dead in his tracks, his eyes wide with fear and suspicion. "I already told you the flute holds the power, this scepter is merely a trinket, a decorative item that helps cleanse my aura."

"Sure," I said, standing up from the chair. "Well, I think I've heard enough. I thought there might be more to it, but you're really just a crazy guy that started a free love cult with a magic item—by the way you shouldn't even be holding that, being a mortal and all, but whatever."

"Sit!" Lyle said in indignation. "I already told you to—!"

With a swish of my hand my magic pulled the scepter from Lyle, it flew across the room and 1 caught it. "Sit down and shut up," I said, deciding to test the scepter for myself. With the instruction Lyle immediately dropped to the nearest futon and went quiet. The cool bronze scepter buzzed as magic pulsed from its staff. "Huh, interesting," I said.

"Chelsea, you are the leader now!" Adina said in adoration.

"No, I'm not. This cult is over, though I'm going to need a little help cleaning up this mess."

Keeping one eye on Lyle I rummaged through my satchel and pulled out my phone. I dialed the number, silently regretting that I had to ask this person for help.

"Hey," I said as the phone connected. "I can't believe I'm doing this, but I need your help with something."

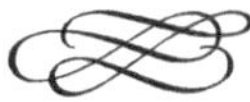

CHAPTER 10

*M*oments later a bright pink cloud of smoke filled the room, and a coughing and spluttering Chad Chaplin emerged from the glittering fog.

"Chelsea, so good to see you! How are things?!"

"Not bad, Chad, you?" I asked.

"Oh, can't complain. So, what's going on here then?" he said as he looked around the decorated room. "This looks intriguing!"

Chad Chaplin was a detective for MCI—Magical Crimes Investigation—and I always loathed to get them involved with anything because they were a bureaucratic nightmare, but this time I genuinely didn't know what I was supposed to do in this situation. I'd never dealt with a mortal illegally possessing a magical item before.

"That guy over there is Lyle Gainsmore," I said, pointing to Lyle. "Though he's been calling himself *Asan Nivon*. He started a free love cult with this," I held up the scepter, "which he stole from Pendle Museum."

Chad looked at the scepter and rolled his eyes. "The Scepter of Anubis! Not again!"

"You know about this thing?" I asked in surprise.

Chad scoffed. "Uh, yeah, The Scepter of Anubis is a royal pain in the butt. This thing has been a minor inconvenience for the MCI since time began. I've only worked at the MCI for a few years Chelsea, and I've come across this little bad boy hundreds of times."

"Wait, what?" I said. "How is that possible?"

"Well around four thousand years ago some ancient Egyptian witch accidentally crafted the first scepter, by itself it's not that troublesome. The scepter has a slight magical charge and in the hands of a mortal they can control and influence others but get this—the charge gets weaker over time until it gets a new owner."

"So that's why the bearded idiot didn't take over the world," I said, looking over at Lyle, who was still sitting silently. "His magic toy was running out of juice."

"Yeah, most cults can actually be traced back to these scepters of Anubis though, they are powerful enough to be bothersome."

"Scepters?" I asked. "As in multiple?"

"Yeah, so that's the annoying thing. Every time there's a full moon the scepter multiplies and its copy teleports to a random location on earth, so there are literally thousands of these things out here, all multiplying every time there's a full moon and arriving at a new location. We have an entire team dedicated to tracking them down and destroying them. There are so many that they slip through our grasp every now and then, like this bad boy."

Chad threw the scepter up in the air and caught it again, like it was nothing more than a cheap baseball.

"So, this thing is a dime a dozen?"

"Yeah, mostly harmless by itself, but its power comes in numbers. We believe the duplication effect was an unintentional glitch, not intended by the original witch that made the scepter. It seems like there's no way to turn it off however, so we're kind of stuck clearing up these things forever. Best to destroy this now—" Chad began, but before he did, I stopped him.

"Wait," I said. "Let's clear up the mess first." I took the scepter back off him and looked at Lyle and Adina. "You're both going to forget what happened in this room. Lyle, you're going to dismantle the cult, sell the building, donate the proceeds to charity and go back to your old life. Return all donations from your followers."

"Yes master," Lyle said blankly, still under the effect of the scepter. I handed it back to Chad, no longer interested in holding this bothersome item.

"Alright, cube this piece of ancient trash."

"Gladly," Chad said. His hands suddenly glowed bright white with magic and the scepter melted into nothingness. "There we go!" he said cheerily. "Another scepter destroyed! If that's everything then I'll just be heading b—"

"What about this?" I said, taking the golden flute from Lyle as well. I was pretty sure the flute was just a distraction to keep people from the scepter, but I wanted to be sure. Chad took the flute and studied it.

"It appears to be made out of plastic, and it says 'Made in China' on the back. I think we're just holding a dollar-store flute." He handed it back to me. "If that's all I'll head off?"

"Actually, there is something else I wanted to talk to you about, if you have a minute," I said.

"What's going on?" Adina said from the couch, rubbing her head in confusion. "What happened in here?"

"Gas leak," I said. "We should probably get out. Lyle, I believe you said something about closing the cult and going back home?"

"Yeah…" Lyle said slowly, also rubbing his head. He stood up and looked around the room as though it was completely new to him. "I'll just go and tell everyone to go home." Lyle left the room, Adina came over to me, still visibly confused.

"So, what was it?" she asked. "How was he controlling people?"

"Turns out there's a Co2 leak in the temple. Yeah, it was built so quickly they cut corners. People were getting disorientated and thought Lyle was some guru because of that. I've just got to catch up with my friend Chad here, he works for the gas company. Can you wait outside a sec?"

"Sure, it'll give me a chance to get down some thoughts about this unusual debacle!" Adina said, following Lyle out of the room.

"Gas company?" Chad asked after she was gone.

"Well, you *are* full of hot air. She's some true crime podcaster, I guess I currently work for her at the moment."

"You've had stranger jobs," Chad commented. "So, what did you want to talk about?"

"Two things really. I was given a powerful book recently, a Magricon—"

"A Magricon?!" Chad said in a hushed shout. "Where in the heck did you get that thing?"

I explained the transfer from Belladonna to myself. "Right… so where is it now?"

"I have it stored safely in a secret vault at my house. I was wondering if the MCI would take it off me. It feels like a dangerous thing to have around."

"No," he said bluntly.

"No? What do you mean, no?"

"I mean no, we're not going to take that thing off you. It's safest in the hands of a High Witch anyway, so it makes sense that you keep it."

"Right… I just thought the MCI might have like ultra-safe places to store dangerous magical items like that."

"We do, but for a Magricon? All bets are off. In all honesty you're best keeping it hidden until the next High Witch appears in seventy years or whatever, then you pass it on to her. Don't do any of the magic in there either, those spells are supposed to be extremely dangerous, raw universal energy—High Witches have accidentally turned themselves into grilled cheese toasties playing around with that stuff. What's this other thing you want to talk about?"

"There's this mad magician, he's taken control of a castle on a small island west of here, and he's trying to take over this island too. It doesn't look like there's a way inside to stop him, he's put up these magical barriers. He's abducting mortals and turning them into strange magical beasts. His name's Mordoc, do you know anything about him?"

"Mordoc… Mordoc…" Chad said, pulling out an unusual looking tablet and typing the name into the device. "Is that with a silent 'g'? No, of course not… ah, Mordoc! Here we are! Yeah, looks like he's on the MCI's most wanted list. You say he's holed up here in a castle on the island?"

"Yeah, and he's actively being a nuisance. Is there anything you can do to help?"

"Um well… you're the High Witch, so to be honest we kind of follow your lead on stuff like this," Chad said.

"What's that supposed to be mean?" I asked.

"We're willing to help, but *you're* the one in charge. I don't know how to put it simpler than that."

"But I'm not part of the MCI!"

"No, but you're more powerful than anyone else in there," he said, staring at me like I was stupid. "Are you not understanding this whole 'High Witch' thing?"

"I… I guess I hadn't really thought about it. Okay, I'll make a plan and then call you when I need you?"

"Pretty much, and if you see any of those Scepters of Anubis knocking around then do me a favor and destroy it on sight! Until next time, Chelsea!" Chad departed in another obnoxious cloud of glittering pink smoke, I fanned away the fumes and walked back through the temple to find disheartened looking followers packing up things and walking out. Outside I found Adina, talking into her microphone as she documented the cult's end.

"Ready to go?" I asked.

"Sure thing. Where to now?"

"Let's go and get something to eat, I think I'm ready to declare this day done."

"Are there many good places to eat here on the island?" Adina asked.

"Oh Adina, you are going to be *pleasantly* surprised. Have you ever heard of Aztec Pancake?"

* * *

THE NEXT MORNING, I woke up early, excited as my fiancé Deacon was due back after being away from the island for the last two weeks.

After his brother had passed Deacon went home to spend some time with his family. His boat was getting in early, so we'd arranged for him to meet me at the house. I'd just finished making breakfast when I heard him open the front door.

"He's back!" Artemis called from the hallway. Before Deacon could even make it into the kitchen I ran into the hallway and jumped on him, smothering him in a hug that was uncharacteristic of me.

"Hey!" he said, catching me with a laugh as he stumbled back a couple of steps. He hugged me back and set me down. "I take it you did miss me then?"

"Just a little bit. I've made you breakfast if you're hungry. How as your trip?"

"It was… well I feel better than when I left. We're all coping with it. I think I'm probably going back to visit mom and dad a bit more often now, maybe once a month or so. Breakfast smells amazing by the way, I'm starving. What have you made?"

"Come see!"

Twenty minutes later we were at the tail end of breakfast, my grand platter of eggs, bacon, pancakes, toast, and other items all suitably demolished. Deacon sat back in his chair, loosened his belt and let out a satisfied sigh as he sipped his coffee. "It's good to be back. So, what have you been up to?"

I caught Deacon up to speed with everything that had happened so far since he'd left the island, from my short stint as a pet detective to the business with the Brewdocks, the Egyptians artifacts, and the cult I'd dismantled yesterday.

"Oh, there's also this other thing, this podcaster is staying in the guest room."

"Another guest? Crikey," Deacon said, pulling a face.

"I know, I know, but this one is fairly normal. She's paying me to be her guide of the island, she actually put me onto an old cold case, I wanted to ask you about it actually."

"Which one?"

"Dec King, the hardware magnate that supposedly killed his wife."

"Ah yeah," Deacon said and nodded his head in recognition. "I worked that case. Guy got off on a technicality, right? As far as I recalled all signs pointed to him doing it. You're trying to prove his innocence?"

"The guy put up a six-figure reward to clear his name, I figured it was worth looking at."

"I see, so what conclusions have you drawn so far?" Deacon asked.

"To be completely honest… right now I think he did it. There was really only one way into that house, using the garage-door opener, and Dec was the only person to have an opener. His wife had one, but hers was broken."

"Exactly," Deacon said. "It's kind of an open and shut case to be honest. No offense sweetie, but I think you might be wasting your time with this one."

"Yeah…" I sighed glumly. "Well, there are plenty of other things going on to keep me busy. How about you? Are you back in work today?"

"Sure am, oops, that's my phone ringing now—" Deacon looked at the phone and rolled his eyes. "It's just Mark and Clark. Probably calling to remind me it's my turn to pick up donuts this morning. Deacon answered the call. "Yes Mark, I know it's my turn to pick up the donuts. Alright, I'll be in the office soon, see you later." Deacon put the phone down again. "That's my cue to leave. I better head back to my apartment and get dressed."

After seeing Deacon out, I went back into the kitchen to clean up. I'd just finished loading the dishwasher when Artemis skidded into the room, slightly out of breath and looking panicked.

"What have you done now?" I asked.

"Not me! The mirror!"

"Which mirror?"

"The magic mirror, on the upstairs landing! It's glowing!"

"Great," I said and rolled my eyes. "Where's Adina? She can't see the mirror acting weirdly." The magic mirror contained a reflection of myself that moved on its own and—for some reason—had a thick New Jersey accent. I'd instructed the mirror to act normally while

Adina was staying here, unless it wanted to get relegated to the attic and covered with a cloth.

"She's in the shower, I could hear her doing some commentary about water running down the drain through the door," Artemis said.

"That's one bonus, we've got at least twenty minutes before she's done with that then. Let's go see why the mirror is glowing."

Artemis ran out the room and I followed him up the stairs to the magic mirror on the landing. Sure enough the reflective glass pane was pulsing with a strange orange light. My reflection was in the mirror, but she was sitting against a wall reading a book.

"What did I tell you about acting normally while we have mortal guests?" I scolded the mirror. In a lot of ways my magic reflection reminded me of a petulant teenager, she was always throwing a strop of some sort, and often acted like she was a victim of great injustice.

"I'm just sitting here reading my book!" my reflection said in her abrasive accent. "What have I done now?!" Mirror Chelsea put the book down in a huff and rolled her eyes at me.

"Well for one you're sitting out in the open. I told you we have mortals in the house. It's kind of an odd look to see a reflection sitting in a mirror when the owner isn't there too."

"She's in the shower! Come on, I've been cooped up hiding, I'm losing my mind in here!"

"The main problem is this," I said, tapping the glowing mirror pane. "Why is the mirror glowing bright orange? That definitely doesn't look normal, even if you are hidden out of the way."

Mirror Chelsea raised a querying brow and then she stood up, walked over to the mirror until she was nearly nose to nose with me and she tapped the glass from her side. "Huh, I have to admit that *is* unusual. Can't say I know what's going on."

"Seriously?" I asked. "This is *your* magic mirror; how can you not know what's going on?"

"Hey lady, it's just as much your mirror too! From where I'm standing, you're the reflection!" *Huh.* I'd never actually thought of it that way before. I watched as the reflection peered at something out of view, like she was fiddling with the frame on her side. "Let's see here… ah, okay looks like someone is trying to contact you. I didn't know that was possible."

"Someone's trying to contact me, through the magic mirror? Who is it?"

"I don't know. Want me to open it?" Mirror Chelsea asked.

I looked at Artemis with uncertainty and he gave me an apathetic nod of his head. "What's the worst that could happen?" he said.

"I don't know, but it usually always seems to happen," I said. "Alright let's answer this call… Artemis, be on standby with magic."

"Sure, sure," he said. Looking over I saw him batting around a piece of fluff with his paw. I rolled my eyes and decided to ready my own magic, Artemis clearly wasn't going to be any help.

The mirror pulsed with one final orange flash and then a quiet 'ding' reverberated through the frame. All of a sudden, the image of Belladonna Brewdock appeared in the reflection, standing alongside Mirror Chelsea. My magical image jumped back in surprise and tripped over on the landing. "Argh!" she shouted. "Someone else is in here!"

Belladonna looked at my reflection with confusion in her eyes then she turned her gaze on me. "You never told me you had a magic mirror," Belladonna said.

"I didn't think it was much of a conversation piece to be honest," I replied. "Mostly she's just a pain in the butt."

Belladonna pursed her lips as though she understood. "That I can attest to. But this is quite handy actually. Magic mirrors act as portals to one another, I have one in my shack on Vassago Isle. It might make getting here a little easier."

"Huh, I didn't know that."

"Yes, that's predominantly what magic mirrors are used for," Belladonna said. "Where did you get this one?"

"I made it," I said plainly.

Belladonna's eyes went wide. "Impressive, even for a High Witch. I tried but could never do it. Mine was inherited."

"How do I use it as a portal then?" I asked Belladonna.

"Stand in front of the mirror and ask the reflection to contact the person you seek. Once they answer, opening the portals is as simple as a mutual agreement. Chelsea, I grant you access, whether I am here or not." With those words the glass rippled, as though a stone had been thrown into water. The reflection of my landing disappeared, and now I saw an unfamiliar room in Belladonna's shack. It looked like the glass was gone now, and the mirror frame was simply a hole in the wall through which I could step.

"Woah," I said.

"Impressive, huh? That was all I wanted to show you. Feel free to use it whenever you want."

"There is something I want to do actually, give me a minute, I need to leave a message with someone." With that I hurried over to the bathroom and knocked on the door. Adina was still in the shower from the sounds of things. I heard her narrating through the door.

"...and like that water our dreams and fears can run down the drain, disappearing into the shadowy—"

"Adina? It's me, Chelsea!" I shouted through the door.

"Am I taking too long?!" she called back.

"No, take your time. I've got to run out and see to something. I'll be back shortly then we can get going about our day. Okay?"

"Okay. I'm going to head into town, anyway, call me and we'll meet up later!"

I ran back to the mirror and wrapped my hands around the open frame, preparing to step through. "Fancy coming along?" I said to Artemis.

"Eh, why not," he said back, hopping through the frame with me.

CHAPTER 11

As I stepped into the shack the smell of salt, damp and decay immediately infiltrated my nostrils. I heard the distant waves crashing upon the rocks outside and saw Belladonna standing in front of the mirror.

"Come in," she scowled at me, her tentacles rolling over the floorboards as she headed out of the room and into the kitchen. "Do you want a cup of tea?"

I opened my mouth to say yes when I remembered the quality of tea last time. "I'll take a rain check thanks, I just had one. Do you have any peanut butter and pickles?"

Belladonna offered me an unsure look. "…Yes?"

"I'll take a peanut butter and pickle sandwich then."

The half-octopus witch looked revolted. "That might be the most disgusting thing I've ever heard. But… what the heck. One sandwich coming up." While Belladonna made the sandwich, I sat down at the kitchen table. Artemis strolled into the room, his bright green eyes taking in the surroundings keenly.

"What a dump!" he said.

"Artemis!" I scolded. "Sorry Belladonna, I didn't realize my familiar was *this* rude."

"Why are you apologizing? This place is a dump," Belladonna said. She brought over my sandwich and set it down. I picked it up immediately and started tearing it apart.

"Still, it's rude to say such things out loud," I said, my mouth half-full of my deliciously gross sandwich. Clearly, I had a few things to learn about manners myself.

Belladonna merely shrugged. "The castle is my home. All the witches in my family lived up there before that crackpot Mordoc turned up and kicked us out. This miserable little shack *does* technically belong to me, but I was never here most of the time. At the moment it's the only thing between me and the sea, so I guess it will have to do. What's with the revolting sandwich combination?" she asked. "Are you pregnant? Seems like a weird craving thing."

"I'm not pregnant!" I said in a panic, a slice of peanut butter slathered pickle slipping out of the sandwich and slapping onto the table. "I just have weird tastes…"

"Uh huh," Belladonna said with a roll of her eyes. "Sure. Just a heads up, but any witch worth her weight in salt can tell when another witch is pregnant. It's very easy to tell."

"I doubt that," I said. "None of the witches in my family have said anything."

"So, you are?" Belladonna said with a smile.

Crumbs on a cracker. "Fine. You've got me. But still, none of the other witches I know have noticed."

"Probably because they're superstitious. Most witches believe it's bad luck to point out that another witch is pregnant."

"Bad luck for me?"

"Bad luck for everyone. I don't believe in that sort of nonsense, and I've just about had my run of bad luck anyway, let's be honest, things can't get much worse for me. Why did you want to come over here anyway? Have you figured out a way to get that miser from the castle?"

"Nothing specific, but I want to try some basic things out, see if I can get *into* the castle first," I said, finishing the last of my sandwich.

"Chelsea's a very busy witch," Artemis said, adopting the air of a boastful secretary. "Just yesterday she broke up a cult and destroyed a scepter of Anubis!"

"Like this one?" Belladonna said, reaching under the table. As she came back up, she was holding—sure enough—another scepter of Anubis. "I use it to prop up the wobbly leg."

"They really are everywhere!" I said in surprise.

"Yeah, they're real pieces of junk, I suppose they're quite dangerous in the wrong hands. Good for propping up tables though."

"…I'm going to have to ask you to destroy that," I said.

Belladonna sighed and put the scepter back under the table. "Will do, at some point. So, what's the plan?"

"Can you show me how to get to the castle?" I asked. "I need to get as close as possible to see if I can get in."

"Sure can. The coastal path will take us to the drawbridge, though Mordoc has had the thing pulled up since he moved in."

"Sounds good to me, show me the way."

THE 'PATH'—AS it turned out—was less a path and more a terrifyingly narrow strip of gravel and rock not much wider than a foot. It started off normally enough but ascended rather steeply, until I found myself following Belladonna along the narrow and winding route up to the castle. On either side of me the earth suddenly gave way to a steep decline that ended in sharp jagged rocks and chaotic white waves.

"Is there a safer path?!" I shouted to Belladonna over the howling wind. Somehow the tentacled squid-witch was traversing the dangerous path with ease, her unhuman limbs rolling over the narrow track with little concern.

"No, this is it," she called back without looking. "Not much further now, it's just up there, see?" Belladonna pointed to the looming figure of the gargantuan castle, which was impossible to miss from any spot on the island. Artemis, who was a few paces ahead of me, didn't seem bothered by the path either.

"It's just a narrow craggy path with a steep fall, Chelsea, what's the problem?" he taunted from ahead.

"I'll remind you of that next time you're stuck up a tree," I said back.

"Hey, that's *completely* different!" Artemis fired back. "Trees are deceptively tricky!"

Ten minutes later I had successfully navigated the winding path without falling to my death. We finally reached the top of the rocky summit and saw the castle properly for the first time. The coastal track ended at a flat plinth of gravel and grass that was about twenty feet square. Beyond this there was a sharp drop to the ocean, and after twenty feet of open air another jut of sharp rock rose up, upon which sat the castle.

Without the drawbridge there was literally no way to get to the castle, the structure was well defended.

"We can't get in without the bridge," I said in realization.

"Nope," Belladonna answered. "Perhaps now you realize the dilemma."

"There are no other entrances?" I asked.

"There are," Belladonna said, "but they're sealed off with magic. There's a dock entrance at the back of the castle, and a few hidden entrances amongst the rock itself, though most of them are only small enough for a bat to get through."

"Bat, why a—" I began, but then I remembered the original owner of the castle was Vassago, it seemed fitting that a vampire would have a couple of bat-sized entrances.

"I've tried to get in every way I know," Belladonna said, "but that jackanape, Murdoc has told the demon to seal off the castle. There's no contending with the magic of a demon."

"Well, let me try," I said. "How does one lower the drawbridge?"

"It's bound to a magical word. *Aperta.* Speak it and the bridge will open, but as you can see—" She held her hand in the direction of the still-closed door. "Zip, zilch, zada."

"Okay, let me try," I said, turning my attention on the door and directing all my magical focus on opening the darned thing. With my fingers ready I felt my power begin to crackle through the air, magical static buzzed through my hair and threads of purple lightning started to frazzle across the ground from my feet. I took a large breath and said the word. "*Aperta.*"

The word rang through the air like the note from a huge bass drum, a wall of force that slowly pulsed outward until it hit the bridge. At once the drawbridge illuminated with shimmering purple light and began to creak and groan. I felt my magic grasp close around the object and I held on tight, pulling as hard as I could, willing the thing to fall down and open.

"Open!" I commanded; my arms now tense at my sides. "Open!" The bridge continued to creak and groan, budging slightly under my force.

"It's moving!" Artemis shouted. Belladonna's mouth opened in amazement as she watched the bridge start to budge. I really felt like I was starting to make progress when all of a sudden, this huge counterforce came out of nowhere and snapped the bridge shut again, the wood slamming in its upright position with a deafening bang that echoed across the island.

The pull threw me forward off my feet and I landed on all fours, out of breath and feeling a little drained of my magic. I scowled, pushed myself back onto my feet and brushed dust and small bits of gravel off my hands.

"That was crazy," I said. "This opposing magical force came out of nowhere and just brushed me aside like I was nothing!"

"That would be Bahmut," Belladonna said sagely, like an elder speaking from decades of wisdom. "Not even a High Witch can contend with the magical power of an ancient earth demon."

I rolled my eyes and grumbled. "Well, this hardly seems like a fair fight. Artemis, do you have any ideas?"

"Yes, I do. Quick question," Artemis put in, "is there anywhere to get food on this rock? A fast-food joint perhaps, or a dollar store?"

"There's a good burger joint on the opposite end of the isle," Belladonna said with a fake smile.

"Really?" Artemis said, his eyes lighting up.

"No," Belladonna said, her mock-hope disappearing from her face. "There's nothing but seaweed and fish. Fill your boots."

"I do like fish…" Artemis mumbled to himself.

"Can we focus a little, Artemis, I'm trying to reckon with the power of a demon here," I pointed out.

"*I* know that, but I'm reckoning with the power of a hungry belly, and I can't get any thinking done without a mid-morning snack."

I sighed and flicked a hand in the direction of the distant ocean below, a second later a half dozen fish appeared over the edge of the cliff, and I dropped them on top of Artemis. "Argh!" he screamed, jumping out of the way of the wet and flopping fish. All but one hopped back over the edge and into the water, leaving Artemis with his impromptu seafood snack.

"Voila," I said. "Don't say I never do nothing for you." While Artemis tucked into his snack, I turned my attention back on the castle and Belladonna. "Any advice?" I asked her.

"Floss daily, but apart from that, no. Your guess is as good as mine, I told you this wouldn't be easy. I'm always a fan of the kitchen sink method. Give it everything you've got, try what you know."

And so, I did. For the next fifteen minutes or so I threw everything I had at the castle, casting a variety of magic assaults that tested the magical fortress from every conceivable angle. My spells and efforts cascaded harmlessly off glowing walls of translucent purple shields, my magic reduced to harmless sparks and fireworks, mere displays of light in the face of this curiously strong demon magic.

I even summoned a broom from one of the shacks on the island, I had this bright idea that *maybe* I could just fly onto the castle rooftop and get inside that way. All seemed well while I was in the air, and I was a few seconds away from actually landing on the castle rooftop when a huge invisible force flung me back in the direction of Belladonna and Artemis, like a magical rubber band pulling me back at the last minute.

I landed back on the gravel flat and dropped to my knees, out of breath and very much drained of my magic. Belladonna approached and helped me to my feet. "For what it's worth the broom thing was very impressive, I haven't seen a witch fly on a broom since I was a child."

"Quite amazing," Artemis said. At first, I thought he was agreeing, but I realized he was commenting on his fresh fish supper. "Nothing beats fish straight from the ocean. Okay, how do we get into this castle?!"

"Are you kidding? I've just been trying for like the last fifteen minutes. It's not happening, this place is impenetrable." As I said those words the image of a man suddenly flickered into view in the air between us and the castle. He was wearing black hooded robes, his white hair was slicked back and fell just above his shoulders, his skin was pale, and his eyes were an unusual yellow color. His face was sharp and angular, handsome in a way, but I didn't find him attractive in the slightest.

"Impressive display," he said casually. "You really are a very gifted witch, but I have to say even your powers are no match for my friend, Bahmut."

"You must be Mordoc," I said. Even from here I could tell this was just an image, not the actual wizard that had locked himself in the castle.

"And you are Chelsea Sponks, the High Witch sent to oust me."

"Pretty much," I said in agreement. "Let's make quick work of it then, open the door and let me in, demonstrate how much stronger you are than me."

Mordoc simply laughed. "Ha! Good one. I already know I'm not stronger than you, but I don't have to be, I've got a demon on my side for strength, I just have to be smarter than you, and all that means is not letting you inside."

"What is it you want exactly?" I asked.

"Is it that hard to figure out?" Mordoc asked. "I simply want to be worshipped by everyone and everything. Taking control of this castle and Pendle Island is the first step to doing that. The magic from the island alone will make me the most powerful wizard in the world, at that point, no one will be able to stop me!"

Although Mordoc was obviously a villain, he wasn't dramatic in the slightest, in fact he was rather the opposite, very calm and composed, like he was giving a sales pitch about windows or something equally as dull.

"Do you take umbrage with that?" he asked.

"I have a problem with you abducting people and turning them into magical beasts. That's a red flag for me."

"The ends will justify the means," Mordoc said in assurance. "Once I've fully absorbed Bahmut's power I'll take the island too. Once I'm in charge there will be no more suffering, no more hunger."

"You could maybe just volunteer at a soup kitchen or something," I said, "but something tells me you'd rather be the center of attention."

"Now you're starting to catch on," Mordoc said with a wry smile. "Be seeing you soon, Chelsea Sponks. Come this full moon I will finally finish absorbing the power of Bahmut, and once that is done nothing will stop me. Ta-ta!"

With that the image of Mordoc vanished. I stood there staring at the empty spot where he had been, listening to the crashing waves below us.

"The full moon is only three days away," Artemis pointed out.

"I'm aware, yes," I said.

"He won't be able to absorb that power without completely losing his mind," Belladonna warned. "How are you going to stop him, Chelsea?"

"Oh, I'll tell you how I'm going to stop him, but just not right now, because I have absolutely no idea," I sighed.

"We're doomed," Artemis surmised.

"Yeah, most likely," I said reluctantly.

CHAPTER 12

After retreating back to Belladonna's house, I made my way into the room with the mirror and prepared to leave.

"I guess I'll be back before three days' time," I said. With the deadline of a full moon approaching, we didn't have much time before Mordoc would become even more of a problem.

"Any ideas how you're going to tackle this thing?" Belladonna asked. Though this was quickly becoming a case of life and death she wasn't outwardly panicked, in fact she seemed rather calm about it all.

"I don't know, it looks like magic isn't working, so maybe I could just get a gun and shoot the bugger," I joked.

"Her fiancé is a sheriff," Artemis pointed out, "she could access the police station evidence room and armory no problem at all!"

"That's always one option," Belladonna said, rolling along with the joke. "Well, come back when you have something, is there anyone else that can help you?"

"The MCI have offered to lend a hand," I said, "though I'm not sure how much help they're going to be."

"Yes, they usually get in the way more than anything," Belladonna said with a note of disinterest. "Well, off you go then, I have to get to my daily sea swim."

I looked at her in horror. "You actually go out swimming in that water? It's freezing on this side of the island!" The water in Delfino Bay was a little warmer thanks to a micro-climate, but everywhere else on the island it was like stepping into liquid ice.

"Swimming in the sea keeps me young, I've done it every day of my fifty years."

"Fifty? You don't look a day over forty-eight," Artemis said cheerily. Belladonna turned her eyes on him and scowled.

"Time to leave now, goodbye," Belladonna sang.

A few moments later I had stepped through the mirror and found myself back on the landing in my home, turning around I saw my reflection in the mirror, painting her nails on the floor. "What?" she asked, automatically on the defensive, "your weirdo friend is out of the house, I don't have to hide."

"I didn't say anything!" I replied.

"How was the trip?" my magic reflection asked.

"Quite handy actually, it turns out I'm utterly hopeless in the face of this mad wizard, though the portals between mirrors are quite handy, that saves me a lot of time. Maybe I should make some more magic mirrors, it would make getting around the island quite easy."

Mirror Chelsea shook her head. "Be careful there Sponks," she said in her abrasive jersey accent, "you can't have too many magic mirrors in one area, three is probably enough."

"Three?" I asked. "Where is the other one?"

The magic reflection shrugged. "I don't know, what do I look like, a magic mirror directory? All I know is that I can feel three magic mirrors, including myself. That Belladonna chick has one obviously, but I don't know who the other one belongs to."

"Could you, like, try and find out?" I asked.

"I'll see what I can do," the reflection said after a moment of consideration. "I'm very busy painting my nails at the moment."

"I can see that..." I said dryly. "Well, I've got nails to paint too. See you later."

I headed down the stairs and found that the house was sure enough, almost empty—or at least I thought it was. It came as quite as surprise then when I opened the front door and saw my gardener, Adam, about to knock.

"Adam!" I said, a little surprised to see him. Adam had a shack at the bottom of the garden, and he lived there most of the time, but he'd been away for the last month or so on other business. "You're back!"

"I am!" Adam was a hulk of a man, a huge lumberjack type, and a gentle giant. "We just came to pick up the last of my things."

I turned my head in confusion. "Your what now?" I asked.

"My stuff, Selena and I have come back to finish moving my stuff out the shack." Suddenly Selena—another former house guest of mine—came into view and smiled.

"Hi Chelsea!" she piped.

"Uh, hi Selena," I said, staring at them both as the penny dropped slowly. "Wait a second, are the pair of you together?" I asked.

They both shared an unsure glance and laughed nervously. "Uh yeah..." Adam chuckled. "Didn't you know that? We're moving in together! I thought you knew!"

"How could I know that? Nobody told me! I didn't even know you were dating!"

"Well, you *are* out of the house a lot," Adam said, "and when you *are* around, you're usually busy with one mystery or another. We didn't want to burden you, you usually have enough on your plate as it is."

"Oh but... I feel like a terrible friend!" I said, an unexpected flood of emotion suddenly coming over me. The last time I cried in public I was seven years old. A seagull stole my ice-cream, and I still hadn't quite recovered from it.

"Chelsea? Are you okay?" Selena asked, her smile changing to a look of concern.

"I'm just so happy for you both!" I blubbered, stepping forward and throwing my arms around them. "You're falling in love and starting a whole new journey together, and I couldn't even take five seconds to notice!"

"In your defense we've been keeping it quiet," Adam said, laughing again as if it was no big deal. It obviously wasn't a big deal, but it seemed that 'not keeping a lid on emotions' was another one of my weird pregnancy things. "Why are you so emotional? I've never seen you like this before. Did something happen between you and Deacon?"

"No, things are better than ever, we're even supposed to be having this stupid marriage soon, if the wedding planner ever gets in touch to let us know what's happening! It's just been an emotional day, that's all!" I said in a blubbering half-shout. I pulled away from both of them and fanned my eyes to stop myself from crying. Selena offered me a tissue and I gratefully took it. "Oh gosh, I have to find another gardener," I said in another moment of realization.

"I'm not quitting," Adam clarified. "Just moving off the property. It's probably time I got out of the bachelor pad. I'm nearly thirty."

A momentary wash of relief came over me as I learned that I wouldn't need to find a new gardener. One thing less on my plate. My phone started ringing, looking at the screen I saw it was Adina.

"Okay, I have to go, I've got a busy day full of nonsense. I'll catch up with you both later, we should go for dinner or something."

"Sounds great," Adina beamed. "Let's arrange something."

I made my way to my little yellow buttercup and answered the call from Adina. "Hey," I said.

"Chelsea? Is everything okay? It sounds like you've been crying."

"I have, but everything is fine. I just got some good news," I explained, taking a deep breath to shift the last of the uncharacteristic hysterics.

"I didn't have you down as the blubbering mess kind of gal," Adina said. "Is the venerable Chelsea Sponks hiding a soft gooey interior?"

"Everyone has a soft gooey interior, that's what makes us so vulnerable. What's up?"

"Just calling to see if you're done with your affairs for the day. I'm in the mood to get back to sleuthing."

"As it happens, I was just about to call you. Where abouts are you?"

"Currently milling about Pendle Mall, can't say there's much of interest here though."

"Well pick me up a soft pretzel or three and get in your van, I've got a plan for the afternoon. Do you have anything fancy to wear?"

"No, but I can pick something up in the mall. Where are we going?" Adina asked.

"We're going to the White Flamingo," I said. "I want to talk to Dec King's wife."

* * *

THE WHITE FLAMINGO was a high-class cocktail bar and restaurant nestled on an upmarket street in the middle of Pendle town. On the way over I used magic to transform my outfit, switching from a regular black dress to something a little fancier. I met Adina on the street outside the cocktail bar, she was wearing a stunning green dress, and I was in royal blue.

"Check us out!" she hollered as I stepped out the car to meet her. "We look like a couple of real housewives!"

"You found that dress in Pendle Mall?" I asked in amazement.

"No, but I remembered about the wardrobe I have in the back of my van. I keep formal dresses in case I need to get into anywhere exclusive—like now." Talk about being prepared. "I love your dress, where is it from?"

I don't know, magic? "Oh, this old thing? It was just lying around at home. How was the mall?"

"Oh, you know, like every other mall in existence. What have you been up to?"

"Uh… stuff," I said, my brain blanking as I failed to come up with a cover for my morning of magical escapades.

"Stuff, eh?" Adina said with a knowing smirk. "If I'd realized it was so important, I wouldn't have bothered you!"

"Sorry, I can't really say, but it is important business, and I'll probably have to spend more time attending to it over the next few days. Anyway, we've got a housewife to interrogate."

"Right, what makes you think she's going to be here anyway?" Adina asked.

"When we said goodbye to Dec at the house he took a call from the White Flamingo, he said his wife, Jennifer, has built a pretty hefty tab here. I figure the odds are pretty good that she's going to be here, if she's built up such a big bill."

"Huh, I must have completely missed that conversation," Adina said.

"No, you were standing there with me, it was a small detail though, not really worth picking up on."

"Yet you picked it up," Adina said, seemingly impressed. "I'm starting to see what separates you from the rest, Chelsea Sponks. Where others see an inconsequential detail, you see potential."

"Trust me, I've followed plenty of inconsequential details thinking they would be important, and they tend to end in a lot of dead ends. I'm not expecting much from this, but let's see what we can dig up. Let's head inside and get a drink."

Adina and I went inside, got ourselves a couple of drinks and sat down at the table. It was just after lunch and the bar-restaurant was about a third full. From our position I could see a few groups of wealthy housewives laughing and throwing back drinks. Now it was just a case of finding the one we wanted to talk to.

"Let me see your file on the case," I said to Adina. "I need a photo of Jennifer."

"I'll do you one better," Adina said, holding up her phone. She was reading some online gossip site, and this particular article featured paparazzi pics of Jennifer King.

"What's this?" I asked her.

"Hardware Queen in gym wear faux pas!" Adina said as she recalled the headline. The 'article' wasn't much more than a dozen photographs of Jennifer taken from across the street. She was walking from a huge SUV to the entrance of a gym. She certainly looked the part of a real housewife, huge blonde hair, thick Russian lashes and enough makeup to sink a ship.

"I don't understand," I said as I looked at the photos. "What's the fashion faux pas? She looks amazing! I can't believe someone would get that dressed up for the gym!"

Adina shrugged and put her phone down. "You know what these paparazzi are like, they try and create a story about nothing. That's what Jennifer looks like anyway, shouldn't be hard to spot her, she certainly stands out."

"How long have they been married?" I asked.

"Two years, they got married a year after Meredith died."

"Huh, seems a little early, doesn't it?" I commented. Perhaps I was being a little judgmental, some people moved on quicker than others.

"I guess now we just play the waiting game..." Adina said, drumming her fingers over the tabletop.

And so, we did. We waited nearly an hour and a half in fact. During that time, I got through several fruity cocktails, all non-alcoholic of course. Adina got bored and started editing some audio on her phone.

I was just about to give up on this poorly thought stakeout and leave when Jennifer finally walked into the bar.

CHAPTER 13

"There, there!" I whispered to Adina, holding up a huge menu and hiding behind it. I put it down a moment later, realizing that we actually had no reason to hide. Jennifer didn't know who we were after all.

Jennifer was with a young man that looked like he worked for some sort of gardening business. The host walked them over to a table on the edge of the room and they sat down. From my current position I could see them perfectly but couldn't hear a thing.

"Ooh, younger man," Adina commented. "Do you think this is an affair?"

"Judging from the way his hand is on her leg, yes, I would say that's a pretty safe bet."

The younger man accompanying Jennifer was very handsy-feely in fact, but whatever their relationship was Jennifer clearly wasn't in the mood. She kept batting his hands away and snapping at him, whatever the problem was, something was bothering her.

"This is a very interesting development," Adina said, keen intrigue evident in her voice. "The wife is having an affair with a younger man. There are more layers to this story than meet the eye." I pulled out the file again and leafed through the pages. "What are you looking for?" Adina asked me.

"Just looking over the notes for Jennifer again, who is she exactly?"

From the notes it appeared that Jennifer had worked with Dec for a number of years. She started off as a regular old retail assistant in his first shop and worked her way up the ranks to become one of his most trusted employees. At the time of Meredith's death Jennifer was working as Dec's personal secretary and assistant, handling most of his day-to-day business. One year after his wife's passing Dec and Jennifer got married in Mexico.

Two years on from that Jennifer appeared to be in the midst of an affair, and by Dec's account his new wife was bleeding the company accounts dry. What was going on here?

While I could focus my magic to improve my hearing, I doubted I'd be able to hear them from here, and I'd spent so much effort trying to get into the castle this morning my magical reserves were already feeling drained at best.

Perhaps there was another way though.

"Anything good?" Adina asked as I looked over the notes.

"Perhaps," I said. "I want to hear what they're talking about, but we can't get much closer without looking suspicious. Do you have any small recording devices that we can plant nearby?"

"Oh boy, now you're asking the right questions," Adina said. She opened up her bag and started pulling out numerous objects. A pen, a small black rectangle, a tiny button no bigger than a cent, a little orb that looked like a fly. Adina shook out her bag and more of the curious objects spilled out onto the table.

"These are all recording devices?" I said in amazement.

"Hey, a good reporter always comes prepared," Adina quipped. "The pen's honestly the best, it gets great audio and blends in well, just click the end and it'll start recording. Drop it on the floor nearby and it'll take care of the rest."

Luckily, I had to walk past Jennifer's table to get to the bathroom. I walked briskly and kept my eyes forward, the pen held down at my side and out of sight. As I passed them, I clicked the pen, threw it under the table behind them and used the last little bit of my magic to soften the landing so it wouldn't make much of a sound. After I was finished in the bathroom I returned to Adina and smiled as I rejoined the table.

"All set," I said triumphantly. "I feel like a spy!"

"Exciting, isn't it?" Adina said. "I don't get to play around with these little toys nearly half as much as I want to. Most of the time I'm cooped up in my home studio recording podcasts about things that have already happened. This is so much more fun… I should do these field investigations more often!"

After that the waiting game continued, but this time we were waiting for Jennifer and her friend to finish their conversation. It turned out we didn't have to wait much longer. The pair were only at the restaurant for fifteen minutes while their tense-looking conversation played out. Jennifer stood up abruptly, whispered something under her breath and then she stormed out, her younger companion quickly following after her.

As soon as they were gone, I jumped out of my seat and ran over to retrieve the pen. As I got back to the table Adina handed me a pair of wireless earbuds and put a pair in for herself too. "Let's see what that was all about then!" she said eagerly, clicking the top of the pen again. The recording started.

"I liked that dress," came the distant but clear voice of Jennifer. "Royal blue, I can't wear that color."

"You'd look good in any color," replied a male voice. This was obviously her friend. "Heck babe, whatever you wear, it looks good on the floor!"

"Shut up Rico," Jennifer said with disinterest. "God, do you ever think about anything else?"

"Hey, relax babe, I'm just trying to cheer you up a little. What's your problem today? You're being a real—"

"Can you ever just sit there and be quiet for a few minutes?" Jennifer scolded her companion. "God if you weren't pretty life would have left you behind a long time ago."

Adina and I nearly fell asleep listening to the recorded footage. For the most part the fifteen minutes of conversation was asinine bickering, absolutely nothing of use that was helpful in anyway at all. It was clear that Jennifer was having an affair with this man—yes—but apart from that there was very little of interest.

"This might be the most boring thing I've ever done," Adina said, looking like she was struggling to stay awake as we listened to the tape.

I laughed. "Deacon said he's done surveillance work before and it's always boring stuff. People aren't nearly as interesting as others imagine them to be."

But then the conversation *did* get interesting.

"Listen, I know why you're in such a bad mood," Rico said after a long and pointless rant about some tv show they both watched. "It's this thing with Dec's wife, isn't it? Him putting up the reward to clear his name?"

Obviously, I couldn't see Jennifer's reaction to this, but I could imagine it based off her verbal response. "Will you shut your mouth!" Jennifer hissed. "I already told you I don't want to talk about that!"

Rico continued, nonetheless. "I'm just saying, I don't like to see you stressed babe. If he's hiring a PI or whatever then maybe we just scare that person off, I can be intimidating when I want to be."

"Are you out of your mind?" Jennifer hissed again. "I've got nothing to hide, I don't care what Dec does, I just want to put this behind us. I thought we were done with this, now he's dragging up the past again."

"Well, his business *is* failing," Rico pointed out. "Guy probably just wants to try and look like he's innocent so he can get customers back in the store again. Doesn't help that you spend all his money."

"Yeah, and who does most of that money get spent on? Stop acting like a spoiled brat, Rico. I can drop you just as easily as I picked you up, there are plenty other men that would like to lay with Jennifer King."

"None of them as attractive as me though, right babe?" Rico said, almost sounding like he was high off his own ego. "It's not my fault your old man won't give you a good time, but hey, Rico is always here to make you feel better."

"All you're doing now is stressing me out, just stop talking and sit there, is that so hard?" Jennifer sighed.

"Look, Dec gave you a good life and all when he was providing, but now that money is drying up and he can't give you what you want anymore. It's not right. I know you Jennifer, you've worked hard to get where you are, the luxury, the life, you deserve it. I know you think I'm just a fling, but I care about you, I do. You need to leave him and get with me."

Jennifer just laughed. "And buy diamonds and pearls on your meager salary? Rico, I make more off the gossip rags than you do from sweating in gardens all day. I don't need a man."

"But you need more money, don't you?" Rico said, an assuming tone to his voice. "Whether you like to admit it or not, you're struggling to keep up with the other women in here, and you're terrified it's all going to go away."

"Just shut up Rico, business will pick up again soon enough."

"When? After this PI proves that Dec *did* kill his wife? Honestly Jennifer you need to get away from that guy, he's a murderer, everyone knows he did it."

"Will you just shut up already?" Jennifer said, her words accompanied by another sigh. "I think this fling has run its course."

Rico laughed in response. "Oh yeah? Well, what if I told you I've got a plan to make all your money woes go away?" he asked.

"I'm listening, and this better not be a darn ponzi scheme."

"A what now?"

"Just talk," Jennifer ordered.

"Well, it's uh… pretty simple," Rico said, lowering his voice. It was difficult to hear now because he was almost whispering, but the recorder just about picked up his voice. "Dec's got that hefty life insurance policy hanging around his neck, right? If something happened to him, that money would go to you, and I'm betting that would set you up for a longtime, maybe even for life—"

"I'm done talking to you," Jennifer said, the cutlery rattling on the table as she slammed her hands down. "Can you even hear yourself? You call my husband a murderer and then you go around and suggest killing him in the same breath?"

"Jennifer, it was just a joke!" Rico said.

"The only joke here is the amount of time I've wasted on you. We're done Rico, done. Don't contact me again."

"Jennifer, Jennifer!" came the distant voice of Rico as he followed Jennifer out of the restaurant. Shortly after that came the sound of my muffled footsteps and the sound of me picking up the recorder and clicking the pen. With the audio done we both took out our earbuds and looked at one another.

"Turns out they had something interesting to say after all," Adina said through a big grin. "What did you make of that?"

"This Rico character sounds interesting, though something tells me he might be all bark and no bite. I think I'll need a copy of that recording nonetheless, I should probably pass that onto Deacon and have his men keep an eye on that guy. Who idly suggests murder over lunch drinks?"

"The idiot that has an affair and falls in love with a trophy wife," Adina said. "It sounds like Jennifer thinks Dec is innocent."

"I got that vibe too. I'd still like to talk to her in person though. I wonder if it's worth calling Dec and seeing if he can set something up." I tapped my fingers on the table as I thought of our next step. "Well, I suppose we better make tracks and get out of here, unless you want to order any more fifteen-dollar mocktails?" I said to Adina.

She laughed. "No, I think I'm good. You head out. I'll pay for the bill and catch up in a moment."

I gathered my things and went outside to the street, jumping back at the last second as I almost bumped into another woman walking in. After a double take, I realized it was Jennifer King.

"Sorry," she said. "I forgot my purse—hang on, don't I recognize you from somewhere? You're the detective woman, aren't you? I've seen your face in all the papers."

"That's me," I said, with my old familiar chuckle. "Guilty as charged. You're Jennifer King."

Jennifer nodded then her eyes narrowed slightly. "Hold on, don't tell me, you're the one my husband has hired to clear his name."

"Well, I'm actually not working for money—yet," I clarified.

"Are you following me?" she said with an air of suspicion.

"No, just meeting a friend here for drinks, she's inside just settling the tab. I *did* want to talk to you though."

"Is that so?" Jennifer said, pushing a hand through her thick blonde hair. "And what is it you wanted to know?"

"Anything you can think to tell me that might help open the case. Was there anything you feel wasn't given proper attention last time around?"

"The whole thing was a mess to be honest, legally speaking of course. I guess the police did a good enough job. The infuriating thing is that Dec gets the short end of the stick. He's innocent in this, he really is!" Jennifer professed.

"So, you don't think he did it?" I clarified.

"No! I mean it all comes back to that question of access, doesn't it? Dec and Meredith were the only ones that could get inside that building. Her remote for the garage door was broken, which meant he was the only that could get in, he had the only other remote."

"But you still don't think he did it, even in the face of that? What's the answer then?"

"Well, isn't that the million-dollar question... or one hundred thousand in this case. Maybe someone took the remote from him and put it back before he noticed. Heck, if you really want to know what I think—" Jennifer looked over her shoulders and leaned in close. "There's an element to this story that has always been ignored."

"And what's that?" I asked.

"Meredith's remote. The only other way to get in."

"But wasn't it... broken?"

"Yes," Jennifer said in a hushed voice. "But she gave it to Dec's brother, Bryan, to get it repaired. There's an expense report for it in the office somewhere, if you look closely enough. I'm sure a woman of your talents could find that piece of evidence."

"I'm confused," I said, my eyes narrowing slightly. "Are you suggesting that Bryan King is the one that killed Sylvia? If you're aware of evidence that could suggest that then you should report it to the police."

"I don't know for a fact it exists; I've just heard rumors on the grapevine. Here's something I do know, Bryan might appear to be gentle and downtrodden, but I can tell you this for a fact, he can be downright scary."

"Scary?" I asked. "Scary how? Are you afraid of this man? Has he threatened you?"

The door leading into the bar opened and Adina walked out. Jennifer quickly composed herself, fluffing her hair out with her hand as she began to walk away. "I've think you've got everything you need from me, Chelsea Sponks. The rest is up to you."

CHAPTER 14

"How are you going to sneak into the office and look for this supposed paperwork though?" Adina asked as we drove back to my house.

"I'm not sure, I mean Dec said I had free reign to go wherever I want, so maybe I could just march straight up to the desk and tell his brother that I'm looking through paperwork."

Not long after that we got back to the house. Adina was meeting up with some other podcasters she knew who were apparently local to Pendle Island, so she headed back out again for her dinner plans, and I curled up in the living room with a book and a cup of tea, and a book about unusual and advanced magic techniques.

"But of light reading?" Artemis asked as he came into the room.

"Just reading about magic mirrors," I said. "Do you know what happens if you place two magic mirrors against each other?"

"Bedlam," Artemis answered. "If a witch is standing between them the mirrors start producing hundreds of copies. The reflections literally walk out of the mirror."

"It sounds cool!" I said.

"Cool and dangerous," Artemis said. "The reflections will be under the witch's control, but if even just one of them refuses to go back into the mirror it could become a big problem."

"Why would they refuse?" I asked. "The book here says that the reflections will obey as long as the with is totally focused."

"Is anyone ever totally focused?" Artemis asked. "Trust me, it's not worth the risk. The last thing we need is another Chelsea running around."

"Just imagine how much I could get done if there was more than one of me though," I said.

After a while I must have dozed off, because when I next opened my eyes, I woke to the sizzling smell of dinner and saw Deacon cooking a meal in the kitchen.

"Evening sleepy head," he said as I walked into the kitchen. Deacon hugged me and kissed me too, I momentarily melted in his embrace, taking a deep breath and savoring his pleasant aroma. "How was your nap?"

"Unplanned," I said. "I don't know why I'm so tired. I feel like I can hardly keep my eyes open at the moment."

"Well, you're walking for two now," he said, nodding at my abdomen. "Running around the island all day is going to tire you out more than usual. Are you in the mood for burritos? I'm cooking up a big batch," Deacon said.

"I think I'm about to fall in love with you all over again," I swooned.

When Deacon finished cooking, we sat down together and ate, talking about our mutual days. Deacon had his hands full with some crazy teenagers chaining themselves to doors outside the town hall. While he told the story I ate four whole burritos.

After that we melted on the couch together and watched TV. It was a nice and calming end to the day, or would have been before a knock came at the door, just after ten.

"I'm guessing that's someone for you," Deacon said, with little note of surprise in his voice. Most people would probably be a little concerned for such a late visit, but it was becoming more common for me lately. "Want me to get it?"

"No, it's okay," I grunted as I pulled myself off the comfortable couch. "Let's face it, it *will* be for me."

I made my way through the kitchen and into the hallway. Pulling open the front door I saw Jack Valentine, my lawyer, and faithful servant of Count Vassago, the vampire that had hired me to get back his castle.

"Chelsea!" Jack said cheerily. "How are things going?!"

"Fine, it's a little late Jack, don't you think?"

"Sorry," Jack laughed nervously. "I'm not much of an early-caller since the whole turning-into-a-vampire thing," he said.

"Fair enough. Well, let's hear it then. To what do I owe the pleasure of this visit?" I said, yawning halfway through the sentence.

"Vassago wanted to know how things are going with the castle. Have you managed to kick the Brewdocks out yet?" Jack asked, his hands twisting together anxiously.

"No, I haven't, and I've actually learned a little more about the situation since going over to the island," I said plainly.

"Oh?" Jack asked. "Like what?"

"Well, the Brewdocks have a different account of events, regarding how everything has gone down. Vassago claimed the Brewdock witches stole the castle from him while he was away travelling the world, but *they* claim Vassago left because the demonic power underneath the castle was too strong for him to bare," I said, recalling what Belladonna had told me.

Jack laughed as though the notion was ridiculous. "Well, that's the thing with witches, you can never tell when they're lying—uh, I mean —" Jack faltered, remembering that I was a witch also. "I didn't mean anything by it!"

"You've gotten a lot worse at talking to women since you became a vampire, I thought you were supposed to be charismatic creatures?" I said with one brow raised.

"It's the darn thirst," Jack explained.

"Thirst?" I asked.

"I'm still technically a fledgling vampire, the first year is supposed to be the hardest. The thirst for blood is all consuming, it's basically all I can think about."

"I see… and are you thinking about that right now?" I said, wondering if I should get ready to blast Jack to kingdom come.

"No!" he blurted. "Chelsea, no! Don't worry, I would never hurt you. I'd never hurt anyone! I already told you Vassago owns one of the largest artificial blood companies in the world. I've got a full supply always ready to go, but it's still very hard to concentrate, it's like I've got this permanent brain fog. Plus, you're safe, I couldn't hurt you even if I wanted to."

"And why's that?"

"Because you haven't invited me in, see?" Jack stepped forward and slapped his hand against the open door. All of a sudden, a bright wall of golden light appeared in the door and blasted his hand away. The force alone sent Jack stumbling down the porch stairs. He caught his balance and spun around again before falling over. "See?" he walked back up the stairs and showed me his hand, which was now charred black. The skin was already starting to rapidly heal itself. "I can't get in, not without an invite."

"Dude that's an extreme demonstration. Are you hurt?"

"No, I'm fine. I'll be all healed up in a few minutes. That's the thing about vampires, they normally trick people into letting them inside."

"Huh…" I said.

"What? Did I say something?" Jack asked.

"Well, you just made me think about the castle problem. I *have* gone over to the island, the last remaining Brewdock witch there says a mad wizard took over the castle and kicked everyone else out. I tried to get in earlier today, but despite all my magic I couldn't do it, this wizard is using the demonic magic under the castle to keep himself locked away, and it's powerful!"

"Huh… I'll report back to Vassago with that then. Is there anything you can do?"

"I've no ideas yet but talking to you may have just opened my eyes. I can't use my magic to force my way in there, but what if I trick him into letting me in somehow. This Mordoc—"

"Mordoc?" Jack asked.

"That's the wizard's name. He said that I'm stronger than him, but as long as he's safe in the castle there's nothing I can do to stop him. But if I trick him…"

"But how?!" Jack said. "You'd have to come up with a pretty good trick!"

"Well fortunately for me I come from a long line of liars and charlatans. Who better to ask than the women in my own family? I'm sure one of my own relatives could help me come up with a cunning and deceptive plan," I said.

"You really think so?" Jack asked.

"Oh, I do," I said with a hearty laugh. "Maybe I can't rely on them for much else, but I know I can count on my family for one thing: deceit and trickery! Mark my words, they're geniuses when it comes to this sort of thing!"

"*Y*eah, sorry dude, I don't have a clue," Lizzy said while we ate a hearty carb-filled breakfast inside Aztec Pancake.

"But your magic is literally fueled by mischief!" I said in wild dismay. "Of all people *you* must be able to think of a way of tricking this wizard into letting us in the castle."

"But *you* already tried to get inside, and even *you* couldn't get in. Like, I can come up with tricks all day long Chelsea, the fact of the matter is that my magical ability isn't as powerful as yours. If you can't get in there, I can't."

"I'm not talking about magic here," I explained. "I'm talking about wits and cunning, and I was under the impression you weren't short of either of those things."

"I'm not sure if that was an insult or a compliment…" Lizzy said, staring up at the ceiling while she pondered it out.

"Let's go with both. The point is that I thought you could offer me another perspective. I'm not talking about magical solutions, I just need to trick my way into this guy's castle before he turns any more people into half-animal-monsters, you saw what he did to Belladonna!"

Lizzy scooped another forkful of pancake into her mouth,

nodding thoughtfully as she chewed down the food. "Yeah, he did turn her into a bit of a freakshow."

"And she's not the only one," I pointed out. "Belladonna said Mordoc has abducted like twenty people now and turned them all into different half-animal monsters."

"Now hang on a moment," Lizzy said. She set her fork down on her plate and wiped her mouth with a napkin.

"You have an idea?" I asked.

"Potentially, but I don't think you're going to like it," she said.

"Cuz, at this point I'm open to anything, let's hear it," I pleaded.

"Okay, so when I was in college, I knew this guy called Tony, he wasn't a great magician, but he was pretty good at illusion, and every summer he'd—"

"Hang on a moment," I said, "What's illusion?"

Lizzy put a hand on her forehead and nodded. "Right, sorry, I keep forgetting you didn't grow up magical, you don't know about these weird little terms. Illusion is like a really weak version of magic, it's kind of what they start kids out with, turning spoons into lollipops, that sort of thing. Nothing actually *changes* with illusion; it just *looks* like it does. It's weak and powerful at the same time, if that makes sense? Like I can use my magic to change this fork into a straw—" Lizzy's fingers danced over the fork and sure enough it changed. "And it's actually a straw now, because I used magic. Illusion would only make it look different."

"Okay, I think I'm with you so far."

"So Tony was this guy I went to camp with, he was a counsellor just like me, we did several summers together. Tony was a nice guy, but like I said, not a very gifted wizard. I mean I'm talking like below average; his magical ability was so weak that he was almost human, but the guy was good at some things. Illusion for example, I never met anyone as good at illusion as Tony."

"What sort of things did he do?" I asked.

"Man, what *didn't* he do?" Lizzy replied. "The thing about illusion is that the spells don't last very long at all, they usually revert back inside a few minutes, usually they don't even last longer than a few seconds, and it's hard to change stuff much bigger than your hand. Tony though, he could make stuff last for days, sometimes even weeks, and not even just that, he could do stuff with illusion that I never saw people do."

"Like what?" I asked.

"He loved making the kids at camp laugh, he'd turn his hands into monkey hands, or give himself a crocodile tail, or a wolf's face—he was really gifted at this stuff, and the kid's loved it. The best thing about it is that the changes reverted back easily, because it was illusion."

"So…where are you going with this exactly?" I asked Lizzy.

"I'm still good friends with Tony," Lizzy said. "He owns a shop over on the maple avenue, the guy is still a practical joker to this day. Not a great wizard, but a great guy."

"How did he get so good at this illusion, but not other magic?" I asked.

"Tony said he didn't have much choice. He wanted to try and keep up with everyone else, but obviously his magical ability just wasn't the same. Most people stop using illusion by the age of ten because you move onto real magic after that, but Tony just kept messing around with it because that's what he did best. I guess those extra few years of practice really helped him develop the skill."

"You think Tony could help us turn back these people that Mordoc abducted?"

"What?" Lizzy said, scrunching her face up at the idea. "No, god no. Were you listening to a word I said? Tony is *not* a good magician, we couldn't put him up against someone like Mordoc, he'd get destroyed! This Mordoc guy seems like a very competent wizard."

"I'm confused then, what is it you're actually suggesting?" I said in exasperation.

"The great thing about illusion is that its magical signature is so weak it's hard to detect when things have been changed using illusion. I think we should go see Tony; he might be able to help us Trojan Horse our way into the castle."

I sat up straight in my chair, finally realizing what Lizzy was suggesting. "Hang on a moment, let me see if I'm getting this right. You're suggesting that we get Tony to use his unusual illusion ability to turn us into half-animals and then sneak into the castle that way!"

"Exactly!" she said excitedly. "It already sounds like this Mordoc character is off the deep end, I'm betting if a couple more people turned up at this door as half-animals, he wouldn't recollect if they were his or not. What do you think?!"

I stared into the distance for a moment as I considered the proposal. It was utterly bonkers, but it was probably just crazy enough to actually work. I mean, I couldn't think of anything more dangerous then voluntarily turning ourselves into these strange half-animal creatures, but at this point what options did we have left?

"I think I like the idea. Do you think we could go and talk to this Tony character now?" I asked.

"I don't see why not," Lizzy said with a shrug. "He's always in his shop, and he's always keen to show off his illusion ability."

"Well let's hit the road then," I said as both stood up from the table, throwing down some cash to cover the bill. "I want to see what this wizard, but not-a-wizard can do..."

I'd spent the last couple of months learning as much advanced magic as I possibly could, but maybe the answer to beating a powerful wizard and strong demonic magic lay in learning basic elementary magic first?

There was only one way to find out.

* * *

Lizzy directed me to Tony's shop, but upon arrival I assumed she had gotten the instructions wrong.

"Uh Lizzy, the sign over the window says, 'Tony's Spreadsheet Consultancy Business,'" I said, stopping short of the front door and staring in dismay at the dismal office interior on the other side of the glass window. Inside I could see harsh office lighting, desks cluttered with paperwork, and corkboards on walls, filled with dreary looking charts and sales figures.

"Oh sweet, naïve, Chelsea," Lizzy hummed as she walked through the front door of the 'Spreadsheet Consultancy Business', stepping inside to the shop. "You are sure in for a treat."

Assuming that my cousin had fully lost it, I followed her inside anyway and let the door close behind me. I looked around at the soulless looking office and took a step forward to follow Lizzy. As I did so the interior started to change, the room transforming before my very eyes.

Over the next couple of steps, the halogen-lit office shed its magical disguise and suddenly became a breathtaking joke shop of epically magical proportions.

The low polystyrene tile ceiling zoomed upwards, turning into a high-vaulted cathedral-like ceiling painted in fantastic candy-striped colors. Every object and surface in the room began to twist and change, tables transforming into cabinets of toys, stacks of paperwork melting into bizarre looking contraptions. When I entered, I had been in a soul-destroying office, but after a few steps I now found myself in a magical joke shop, my eyes captivated by its countless shelves of intrigue.

"If it isn't Lizzy Sponks herself!" a man said, appearing from somewhere at the back of the shop. He had a huge white beard and magical robes that looked like they had been dipped in a rainbow. The garments shimmered and sparkled as he walked forward, colorshifting smoke wafting off his shoulders as he came closer. "And I recognize you in an instant," he said, setting his unusual golden eyes on me. "Chelsea Sponks, the island detective. My name is Arazmo, pleased to meet you."

With his introduction 'Arazmo' produced a bouquet of flowers in my direction, offering them to me. I went to take them, and they transformed into a flock of pink doves. The doves flew up towards the vaulted ceiling, turning into falling petals as they ascended. The petals fluttered down through the air and froze in place.

"Quite the introduction," I said.

"Stop showing off!" Lizzy laughed. She walked forward and gave 'Arazmo' a playful punch in the arm. "Chelsea this is my friend Tony.

Pay no attention to the 'Arazmo' business, that's just one of his many characters."

"Characters?" I asked.

"Why, there's no fun in spending your life as one person," the rainbow-draped wizard said to me. "Why not be as many as you like, spend a different day as someone new? Open your eyes to the perception of the world."

With that 'Arazmo' gave a playful flourish of his hands and a vortex of magical wind swept around him, transforming him from a bearded man to a tall brunette woman in sweats and a hoodie, and a dusty blue apron.

"You've got me, Toni's the name, and illusion is the game. Care for a mocha-frappe-latte?" 'Toni' gestured in the direction of the shop and in the blink of an eye the magical toyshop transformed into a chic-looking coffee shop. The change was so vast and effortless that it left me feeling a little dizzy.

"How on earth did you—" I began.

"Or maybe you want something a little more mystical?" 'Toni' said as she walked through the aisles. In another blink of the eye the shop and he—or her?—transformed. We were now standing in an oriental apothecary, and 'Toni' was now a miniature and ancient Asian man in red silks.

"My name is Fe," he said, "Would you like some tea?"

Lizzy just rolled her eyes and laughed. "Are you done showing off, Tony?" she asked.

"Showing off?" 'Fe' said. The small Asian man twirled his long white moustache and laughed. "Who said anything about showing off? It's not every day a High Witch walks into your shop. I'm just trying to entertain!"

'Fe' clapped his hands together. The shop transformed again, becoming some sort of supplement store. Fe was now a huge and muscular black guy in a tight tank top. "You've got to remember that fat is *not* the enemy. Tyson's the name and getting shredded is the game."

With another clap of his hands the shop transformed into a guitar shop. 'Tyson' was now a small Latino girl with a pink mohawk, holding a cherry pink guitar. She slammed out an insane guitar solo and gave me the horns.

"Of course, this is all a little derivative," she said. "If you really put your imagination to it, you can go anywhere."

The small Latino girl snapped her fingers and suddenly we were on the middle of a floating platform in a stormy sea. I dropped to the wood to stop myself from falling into the raging ocean. The platform was cold, wet, and slippery. Cold sea spray bit against my face and the wind howled all around us.

With another snap of her fingers the scenery changed again. Thus came a rapid-fire shift of scenery, all with encompassing sensory detail that made it feel unwholly real. Blazing desert, arctic tundra, a seabed swimming with thousands of sharks. The magical tour ended seemingly in the midst of space, starry canopies surrounding us and colorful galaxies stretching for thousands of lightyears beyond my eyes.

"This one is my favorite," came a gentle voice. Looking over I saw a regular man in a t-shirt and jeans. He was of average height, with short brown hair and dark brown eyes. "It's quiet up here, and the view is quite spectacular."

He gestured for me to turn around and I did, floating in the seeming anti-gravity of space. There below us I saw the earth, or a magical vision of it at least. A vast ocean of calming blue surrounded me, and I felt strangely at peace. I knew that none of this was real, I'd just been on a whirlwind tour of Tony's breathtaking illusion magic.

"I'm Tony," Tony finally said, holding his hand out and shaking mine. "Welcome to my shop, I hope the tour didn't startle you."

"Not at all," I replied. The space setting receded, and all of a sudden, we were standing in the dreary-looking office again, bright halogen lights overhead and office tables piled with paperwork surrounding us. Tony was still a man of average height with brown hair and dark eyes, but he was now wearing a suit. "That might be the most impressive display of magic I have ever seen," I said.

Tony blushed and laughed nervously. "All just creative illusion.

Not much magic to report honestly. I'm not what most people would call a gifted magician, hence my regular day job." Tony motioned to the office around him. "I crunch numbers by day and peddle magic tricks by night. People call me Spreadsheet Tony, I'm a wizard when it comes to *that* sort of thing."

I shook my head in disbelief, looking at Lizzy and Tony in turn. "Not a gifted magician? I think you might just be the most powerful magician alive."

Tony laughed again. "I am humbled by your compliments, honestly. Truthfully though my magic doesn't have much use beyond illusions. Illusion is mostly seen as a tool to educate younger witches and wizards; it's practical purposes are few and far between."

I looked at Lizzy. "Is the entire magic world mad? How can people not be impressed by this?"

"People *are* impressed," Lizzy clarified. "But Tony is right, there are limits to what he can do with his magic."

"But I can't tell what is real and what's not real!" I said. "Is this office real?"

Tony smiled. "Now that would be telling, wouldn't it? So, what brings you both to my shop? It's not every day a High Witch comes into my life."

"There's a castle on a small isle west of here," I said to Tony. "A mad wizard has taken over it, and I need to get inside, but it's proving a little difficult. Lizzy seems to think you might be able to help."

Tony laughed nervously. "Me? What can I do?"

"Your illusion," Lizzy said. "We were hoping you could change our appearance, help us slip inside the castle."

"There are plenty of real spells that can change your appearance," Tony said. "They'd be more powerful than illusion, and they'd last longer too."

"We can't use magic until we're inside," I said. "The wizard in the castle, he'd be able to detect the magical signature, to fool him the effects have to be indetectable. Lizzy told me that illusion produces almost no signature at all." Even just standing there in the shop I could hardly feel the familiar crackle of nearby magic energy on my fingertips. I blinked to activate my witch sight, and the only lines of magic I saw were coming from myself and Lizzy.

"So, you need to look different, and that change has to be imperceptible," Tony surmised.

"That's exactly right," I said. "Do you think you can do that?"

"Hm…" Tony folded his arm and tapped a finger against his chin. "How many people are we talking here, and how long does the change have to last?"

"How many people do you think could handle at once?" I asked him.

Once again Tony thought about it. "Maybe five. And I could maybe give you five minutes total. Would you need more than that?"

"No, I'm willing to work with whatever we can get at this point."

"What do you need to look like?" Tony asked. "Are we talking drastic changes here, or simple things like hair color and facial features?"

"Uh…" I looked at Lizzy and she looked at me.

"You need to turn us into half-animal monsters," Lizzy clarified.

Tony raised his brow in intrigue and chuckled. "Right, just everyday run of the mill magic then, eh? What kind of monsters?" I told Tony what Mordoc was doing to the people he abducted. So far, I'd only seen two of his gruesome experiments, Belladonna, and the half-man half-stag I'd seen in the woods a few months ago.

"What do you think?" Lizzy asked Tony. "Can you do it?"

"I can give it a shot. Did you have any particular animals in mind?"

"Gorilla arms!" Lizzy shouted without missing a beat. Tony and I both stared at her in bemusement. "What? They're super strong. It would be fun."

"I don't see the harm in a dress rehearsal," Tony remarked. "Let's see what I can do." With that Tony turned his attention and Lizzy, took a calming breath and blinked. He didn't raise his hands or move in any noticeable way. Magic usually came with a crackle in the air, or a rush of wind, but I felt nothing at all, it was… very unusual.

But all of a sudden, the change came over Lizzy. A huge pair of gorilla arms hulked out of her dress, ripping the fabric from the shoulders down. Lizzy gasped in amazement and swung the arms around, knocking over a table and accidentally smashing a hole in the wall as she did so. "This is amazing, Tony, I'm—oops sorry!"

Lizzy suddenly pulled the arms into her chest, staring at the huge hole she had pounded in the wall.

"Sorry for what?" Tony asked. "It's just illusion, remember?"

With a blink of his eyes Lizzy's arms returned to normal again. The hole in the wall vanished and the table she had knocked over looked perfectly fine. "You fixed the damage!" I remarked.

"There was never any damage to begin with," Tony clarified. "It was just illusion." Man, wrapping my head around this was going to take some getting used to. "What about you? What would you want?"

"I'm not sure, but my face needs to be obscured. He recognizes me. Same for Lizzy too, actually."

With a nod of his head, I suddenly felt a change come over me. I glanced myself in a mirror on the wall and saw I was twice the size as before, with a bear's head, and bear legs. I opened my mouth to speak but only a large roar came out. Tony offered another minute nod and the change reversed.

"That was amazing!" I gasped. I still couldn't believe none of this was actually happening, Tony *was* a gifted magician, even if he didn't think so. "You can really do that for five people?"

"For around five minutes, yes. It's harder to sustain illusion on other folks, and even more so outside of my own personal space. I'm confident I can give you a little advantage though."

"That settles it then," I said to Lizzy. "I think we might have a way in."

Now I just had to come up with a plan for defeating Mordoc once I was inside.

CHAPTER 16

"How were your errands?" Adina asked me as she climbed out of her van. We had both pulled up in the parking lot of the strip mall, ready to venture into Dec King's hardware store once again.

"Not bad," I said. "I think I'm making progress. How was your meetup?" I asked her. Adina had gone for lunch meetup with some fellow podcasters.

"Not… great," she said with a sigh. "It turns out they weren't really podcasters. I mean one of them has a show, but they only have like three episodes. They were all fans in disguise, just looking for an excuse to grab lunch with me."

"That sucks, sorry."

"Eh, it wasn't all bad. I figured I should make the most of a bad situation and see if I can get any footage out of them. Everyone has a hometown murder story that they want to share."

"They do?" I asked.

"Oh yeah. I have a regular segment on my podcast that's dedicated to hometown murders. Listeners send them in, and I have my producer go through them to see which ones are worth the airtime. Most of the fan mail I get is regarding hometown murders."

"Seems like everyone is murdering everybody out there," I commented as we walked across the lot and approached the automatic doors of the hardware store. They didn't open, and from a placard on the wall I saw that the shop was closed.

"Drat," Adina said. "Have we missed our chance to snoop around today?"

"I think we'll be fine," I said. "Dec said we have unlimited access, wherever, whenever we want. I'll give him a call." I pulled out my phone and dialed Dec. He answered almost straightaway.

"Tell me you've cracked it," he said, an air of tiresome desperation on his voice.

"Still working on it. I wanted to have a look around the office at the hardware store, see if I can dig anything up. We're outside now but its closed, is there any way we can get inside?"

"Go around the side of the building and you'll find a service entrance, there's a buzzer on the door. Susan is always the last in the building, she works late taking care of admin and paperwork. I'll call her while you walk around and tell her to let you in. Any answers yet, Sponks?"

"None yet, but you'll be the first to know," I said. "Goodbye."

"Bye," Dec said gruffly as he hung up.

Adina and I walked around the side of the store and found the service entrance. The door opened almost as soon as I pressed the buzzer and I saw Susan, Dec's assistant standing on the other side.

"Come in," she said. "Dec just called to say you were coming around." Susan stepped to the side and we both came in. She closed the door and smiled. "So, how's the case going?"

"It's moving along nicely," I lied. "We're just here to look through some old paperwork."

"Oh?" Susan with a note of interest. "Anything in particular that I can help you look for?"

"I work by intuition mostly," I said. "If you can just guide us to the main office and the area where you store your paperwork, I'll be happy to take it from there."

"Of course, follow me," Susan said. With that we both followed her down stark concrete hallways until we reached the office a minute later. Susan pointed out the main cabinets for paperwork before dismissing herself. "I'll be in my office down the hallway. I'm usually there for another hour or so. If you need help finding anything, just call. You're not… you're not going to make a mess, are you? I have a very organized system. If you let me know what you're looking for—"

"I'm afraid that's confidential at this time," I said. "But I'd be interested in knowing where you store expense reports."

"The cabinet over there by the printer," Susan pointed. "That large black binder on top is an inventory of all the paperwork too. If you need to find something then look there first, it will tell you where it is."

"Very organized," I commented.

"I like to keep on top of things!" Susan laughed nervously. "Help yourself to coffee and tea." With that Susan left the room, returning to her own private office. Once she was gone Adina turned to me, her microphone held up in the air.

"What are we looking for then, chief?"

I waited a moment before answering, making sure that Susan was in fact gone. I didn't exactly like spelling out every word of my internal monologue, especially when I was trying to figure something out in secret, but as I was technically working for Adina, I figured I owed her one good soundbite at least.

"After my run in with Dec's wife, Jennifer King, she gave me the impression that we should be looking at Dec's brother, Bryan. Jennifer seemed to suggest that Bryan was the one that had the spare garage door opener, meaning he had the only other way of getting into the house."

"So, Bryan is our main suspect?" Adina said with interest and surprise. "But what motive would he have for killing his own brother's wife?"

I shrugged. "Honestly, I don't know, right now I don't have any motive. If I was making surface-level judgements off the top of my head, then I think we have to look at the sort of relationship that

Bryan and his brother have." I walked over to the cabinet that Susan pointed out and opened the top drawer.

"What do you mean by that?" Adina asked, following me with her microphone held up high.

"Well, I've seen the way that Dec and Bryan speak to each other. Dec is the breakaway brother, he found a lot of success, made a name for himself and established a successful business empire. He employed his own brother to help him out, and Bryan seems to have his own ideas about the business, but Dec dismisses them without even listening. I can imagine that might stir some resentment."

"So maybe he killed the wife out of rage?" Adina suggested.

"I think we don't have enough information to make any guesses yet," I said. "But Jennifer seemed convinced the answers lie in the paperwork within this office. I'm inclined to dig around and see what I can find out."

And dig around I did.

Over the next forty minutes Adina and I leafed through endless reams of paperwork, our eyes beginning to droop closed as we scoured the most boring expense reports ever known to man. It seemed like everything we came across was completely irrelevant, order reports for industrial paint orders, sales charts for specific promotional schemes, it was, in three words—dull as dishwater.

"Okay Chelsea I'm having trouble keeping my eyes open here," Adina said, putting another folder back and closing the cabinet she was standing in front of. "I hate to say this, but if things don't get interesting soon, I'm going to have to cancel this episode of the show. This mystery is turning into nothing!"

"Geez Adina, talk about turning up the pressure. Don't worry, something always turns up, and something exciting always happens." A few seconds of silence passed between us and then a loud noise made us jump. After a brief moment of panic, we realized it was the fax machine.

"Oh, look at that," Adina said as the fax came through. "A sales report about cabinet handles. This is really thrill a minute stuff, Chelsea."

"Hey, I'm just looking into this, okay? The universe is the one throwing the curveballs my way…it just seems it's not doing much pitching at the moment." With a sigh I opened another cabinet draw and let my fingertips walk along the edges of folders. I stopped at one randomly and pulled it out. It appeared to be a ledger for the company credit card, right around the time that Dec's wife was murdered. I opened the folder and let my eyes wander over the lines and lines of numbers.

"Alright I'm calling it," Adina said. "I'm packing up and—"

"Hold on a second," I said, putting my hand in the air to silence Adina. "I think I might have something here. There's an invoice here from an electronic repair shop, the item is for a garage door-opener, and look at the name on the invoice, it was signed by 'Brian'."

Adina's mouth opened. "Wait a second, so Bryan repaired the garage door-opener, then that means he *did* have access to the house. That means he must have been the one that did it!"

I closed the folder, twirled it through the air in triumph and caught it again, recognizing the misspelling straightaway. "Don't be so hasty. Let's wrap up, I think we have our—"

All of a sudden, a scream rang out through the building, and as be both turned in that direction, I saw a masked figure holding a gun. Without warning they fired at us. I threw up an invisible defensive shield with my hand, dived at Adina and we both hit the ground, covered by a desk.

"We hit the ground, bullets flying through the air as a mysterious masked assailant tried to take our lives!" Adina said excitedly as she pulled out her microphone.

"Good lord you don't miss a chance, do you?!" I said, jumping up onto my feet and peering over the desk. I saw the masked assailant take off down the corridor.

"Wait, where are you going?!" Adina shouted.

"I'm going to catch this shooter!" I said. "Stay here and stay out of the way!" I started running in the direction of the fleeing gunman. "Hey! Get back here!" I said. "Where do you think you're going?!"

Gun or not, this person had picked the wrong day to mess with me.

* * *

"Help!" I heard Susan shouting as I ran down the corridor after the shooter. "Help, help!"

I passed her door and saw her on the floor clutching her leg. After a moment of indecision, I decided to run in and check she was okay.

"What happened?" I asked.

"I'm shot! In the leg! Call an ambulance, call an ambulance!"

"Adina!" I shouted at the top of my voice, hoping the words would carry. "Call an ambulance, Susan is hit!"

"On it!" Adina's faint voice shouted back.

"We need to tie this off," I said. "Close your eyes." Susan did as I said. With her eyes closed I conjured up a piece of hose and tied it around the top of her leg to stop the bleeding. Susan opened her eyes again and her brow knit with confusion.

"Where did you get that?!" she asked in alarm.

"Never mind that. Keep pressure on the wound." I jumped to my feet and headed for the door.

"But where are you going?!"

"Catching this madman!" As I ran into the corridor, I saw Adina running toward Susan's room, with her phone pressed against her ear.

"Stay with her, make sure she's okay!" I ordered.

I started running as fast as I could, adopting the best sprinter stance an amateur runner could. I'd come across a spell recently during my studies and decided this would be the best time to try it out. As I ran, I whispered the incantation under my breath. I didn't feel like I had a lot of magic left, so I had to make every word count.

"Eyes of a tiger, ears of a bat, legs of the cheetah, grace of a cat."

I felt the warm spell bloom within me, suddenly elevating my senses to superhuman levels. Colors and lights swelled all around me, and I heard the distant footsteps of the fleeing gunman. A surge of strength and speed flourished through me too, my stride growing longer and my feet almost seeming to glide over the floor. I reached a corner, skidded around it like some sort of superhero and saw the gunman fleeing at the other end of the corridor.

Oh no you don't!

Another burst of speed came over me and I shot down the corridor like an Olympic athlete, closing the distance twice as fast as I usually would. The gunman had burst through a door into the shop floor and as I came through the door, they started shooting at me again. Bullets ricocheted off concrete and metal, and I cast more magical shields to send the bullets wayward.

"Get back here!" I shouted. The gunman ran through doors that led into the warehouse and I followed. As I came through the warehouse doors, I saw a black blur flying towards me in the air, it was the shooter's pistol. The gun hit me square in the forehead and I dropped straight to the ground, not having enough time to defend myself with magic.

"Cheap move!" I groaned and pushed myself back onto my feet. I grabbed the gun without thinking and carried on after the shooter, who was now running up a stairwell that ascended the height of the warehouse. I tore up the stairs, almost completely out of breath as I reached the door at the top.

The door opened out onto the roof of the giant hardware store, I saw the shooter tearing across the galvanized metal roof and I gave chase. I was out in the open now and could use magic to trip them, but I just had to get a little closer.

"Stop running!" I panted. "I am in no mood for any more exercise today!" I jumped onto the metal roof and started chasing the gunman, my magically heightened stride quickly closing on theirs, I lifted a hand to blast them with magic but as I went to conjure the spell I felt a weak glimmer that indicated my magic was spent. *Argh!*

With no other way to apprehend the shooter I threw the gun that I had picked up, which had hit me in the head only seconds earlier. I wasn't particularly a great shot, but perhaps the magic spell heightening my senses was on my side. The empty gun cartwheeled through the air, smacked the assailant on the back of their head and they dropped to the galvanized metal roof with a grunt, all fight leaving them as soon as they hit the aluminum paneling.

"I think that's enough, don't you?" I said, forcing one last bit of magic to bind their legs and arms with rope. I got closer, pulled off the black balaclava covering their face and gasped. "Jennifer King?!"

"Untie me now, you wench!" Jennifer barked at me. "I'll have you arrested for this!"

"Only one of us is getting arrested here sugarplum, and something tells me it ain't me."

"I'll have your head for this, you hear! You can't treat me like this!"

"Oh, I think you'll find I can." I pulled out my phone and called Deacon. He answered on the first ring.

"Italian or Chinese for dinner?" he asked.

"Chinese," I said. "Also, I need you to come down to the hardware store and arrest someone."

"Are you okay? Is this the Dec King thing?"

"Yeah, I think I've solved it. What do you know, it wasn't him, it was his old secretary—who is now his wife."

"I'm coming right now. Where are you? Is she apprehended?"

"We're on the roof, and yeah. See you soon." As that call ended, I made another one, to Dec himself.

"Look Sponks I already told you, you have unfettered access to—"

"Make the check out to Chelsea Sponks. The case is done and dusted," I said.

"You're kidding?! Who was it?!" Dec said, his voice animated.

"Jennifer. She just came in here and tried to kill Susan, me, and Adina. I think I know what happened, but something tells me she'll spill it all before she gets taken away."

"I'll be over right now, hang tight." I ended the call and looked back at Jennifer.

"You've got it all wrong!" she barked. "You're going to jail for this!"

"Oh, shut up," I said with a sigh.

CHAPTER 17

Half an hour later Jennifer King was handcuffed in the back of Deacon's police cruiser, Susan had been carted off into the back of an ambulance and taken to hospital—it looked like she was going to be okay thankfully—and the lot outside Dec King's hardware store was a theatre of frivolity and excitement, news crews, reporters, and emergency services as far as the eye could see.

A golden limo pulled to a stop in the parking lot, and everyone scrambled at once for a soundbite as the passenger climbed out—it was Dec King.

"Get out my way!" he said dismissively, batting his way through the crowds of reporters as he made his way over to me. Deacon had his men cordon off the scene with police tape, which thankfully kept the reporters out of the way, they will still lurking on the sidelines like vultures however.

Deacon waved Dec through the police tape. He marched right over to me, put his hand in his pocket and pulled out a check book. "I have to give it to you Sponks," King said as he made out the check. He tore it out of the book and handed it to me. "I didn't think anyone would actually be able to end this nightmare." He looked over to the cruiser where Jennifer was currently cuffed in the back.

"Let me hear this sweet conclusion then. What the hell happened here?"

"It's Jennifer, Dec. She's the one behind all this."

Dec threw his head back and laughed, but the laughter didn't last long. A disbelieving look came over his face and he scowled at Jennifer in the back of the cruiser. "I can't believe it; she's been under my nose this entire time. I married my wife's murderer."

"Still," Deacon said. "At least your name is cleared now."

"That's true," Dec said, though the notion seemed to bring him little relief. "I have a lot of bad business to put behind me. That demon woman ruined my life, and she nearly destroyed my business too. Thanks to you Sponks my name is clean now. Hopefully the people of this island will start shopping at my business once again."

"With a little bit of crafty sponsorship, they just might," Bryan said as he slipped in from the crowd. "I heard what happened, I can't believe it was Jennifer all this time. How are you holding up brother?"

Dec sighed but looked happy to see his brother, they approached one another and hugged briefly. "I'll be glad to say this is all over. We've got a business to rebuild, and you're right Bryan, a couple of TV spots will do us just fine."

Bryan shook his head. "I've already got one better for you, Dec. I found us a new sponsor, their listenership is massive, and the advertising rates are decent too."

"Listenership, what are you talking about? Radio? Who?" Dec said in confusion.

Bryan waved his hand and Adina stepped over. "What do you say? We can work out some discounted rates if you'd like to advertise on the internet's largest true crime podcast."

Dec stared between the two for a moment. "You know what I can't profess to understand these internet radio shows, but what the heck, let's do it. Bryan... set it up." Dec turned his attention back on me, his eyes bright with anticipation. "So, tell me what happened then."

"It all clicked into place once Jennifer pointed me in the direction of Bryan. It became apparent fairly early on that the killer had to have had one of the two garage door-openers, they were the only way into the building. You had one of course, that's why you were the main suspect for so long. But the other one, well—everyone assumed nothing of it because it was broken."

"Right, so how did that succubus break into my house and kill my wife?" Dec asked.

"It's very simple. She repaired the thing. Jennifer was actually the one that put me onto the task. She had repaired the garage door-opener as part of her assistant work for your wife at the time. Jennifer had a habit of spending too much on her corporate card though, so it was maxed out. Here's the part that you didn't know about, she and your brother had a secret arrangement."

"Hang on a second," Bryan said as he stepped into the mix. "What are you talking about? We didn't have any sort of secret arrangement. Dec, I'm not having an affair with Jennifer, I promise!"

"Not an arrangement like that," I clarified. "But you were soft on her Bryan, you knew that Jennifer was routinely short on her corporate card, so you let her use yours, as long as she put the receipts in your name, but here's the thing—she always misspells your name as 'Brian'. The receipt for the clicker repair had your misspelled name, so it had to be Jennifer that did it."

"That arrangement wasn't exactly secret," Dec said. "I told Bryan to help Jennifer out if she was short."

"But it was the crucial bit of evidence that you all forgot about, except for Jennifer of course. She knew the receipt for the repair was a smoking gun, so she didn't say anything all this time. Jennifer didn't want to implicate Bryan; he'd done nothing wrong. She got lucky that the prosecution overlooked that little tidbit."

"I don't understand though," Dec said. "Why did she change her tune now? You said she told you to look through the paperwork. That sounds like she was trying to frame Bryan."

"Because you reopened the investigation," I said. "By doing that you turned up the pressure. Jennifer knew we would get close to her eventually, so she pointed me in the direction of the paperwork that would make Bryan look guilty. She forgot to account that she misspells his name though, highlighting that it had to be her that wrote the receipt. As soon as I saw Bryan's name on those forms, I knew that he was innocent, and I knew Jennifer had to be the one that set him up. She saved me another job when she burst into the office with a gun, I guess the stress just got to her."

"But why do it in the first place?" Dec said in exasperation. "Jennifer and Meredith were friends. Why would Jennifer do a thing like this?"

"For the insurance payout that you received three months after Sylvia died. From looking over accounts it appears that the majority of that payment went right into her pockets, to fuel her uncontrollable spending habits."

A grave look came over Dec's face and he nodded solemnly, as if finally accepting the facts. "Get her out of here, I don't want to look at her again."

As the cruiser pulled away Deacon dismissed the rest of the reporters until there was only me, Deacon, and Adina left outside the hardware store.

"Right, I'll go get the car and we can head home," Deacon said. "Wait right here, I'll be back in a second."

"Sure thing," I said, kissing him as he left. Once he was gone Adina turned to me.

"I can't believe you actually did it, Chelsea Sponks," Adina said. "I suppose I should never have doubted you. Thanks for saving my life back there by the way. You know it's crazy… but I could have sworn for a moment in there you made those bullets move out the way with your own hands."

I laughed nervously. "I… what?! No, that's crazy, your mind must have made that up in the heat of the moment. Adrenaline is one heck of a drug!"

"Yes, I'm sure," Adina said with a smile. In that moment it was like a change came over Adina, her demeanor and expression all changing in a slight way that was imperceptible, but somehow made her seem like a completely different person. "You know you're a very gifted witch, especially for someone that has only been involved with magic for such a short time. There is potential in you, it's raw and rough around the edges, but I think it can be shaped into something truly brilliant."

My mouth was hanging open in response, my head turned as I looked at Adina in disbelief. "You uh… you know about magic?"

With that Adina gave a flourish of her hand and a small cyclone of orange sparks twisted through the air. In her outstretched hand there was a small card. She gave it to me, and I read it.

Adina Lopez, Agent 373. M.A.G.E.

"Mage?" I asked, curiousness taking over me completely.

"Magical Agency for General Enigmas," she explained. "Not many know about us, but now you do."

"What do I do with this?"

"I'd drop it if I were you, it's going to self-destruct in the next five seconds."

I dropped the card and as it fell through the air it disappeared in a burst of fire, turning to ash and smoke. I looked up at Adina. "You're not human, are you?"

She smiled and as she did, I blinked to activate my witch sight. At first there was no magical presence around her, but then a flurry of invisible purple lines appeared in the air, turning all around her like waves around a magnet. I blinked away my sight.

"You can hide your magic?" I asked.

"All good witches can, with a little bit of practice. No one else hears about this conversation, do you understand? It's all very top secret. You're in the know now though, and I wanted you to know that MAGE has its eyes on you."

"Is that a good or a bad thing?" I asked.

"It's good, very good. We're good guys, Chelsea, and we're always looking to recruit more. We only accept the top witches and wizards though, and I think you might just make the cut. Have a think about it and let me know. We'll be in touch."

"Okay…" I said, looking across the lot to see what was taking Deacon so long. I then realized he was only about two dozen footsteps away from us, frozen in time as he headed for his cruiser. I looked back to ask Adina if she had frozen time around us, but when I did, she had disappeared. I heard Deacon's footfall resume and saw him in motion again. He brought the car over a moment later.

"Where's Adina?" he asked.

"She uh… had to go," I said, still feeling very confused about the whole thing.

"Fancy a police escort home?" he asked.

"Sure thing," I grinned. Deacon pulled away, waiting for me in his cruiser at the edge of the parking lot. I made my way over to my little yellow buttercup, wondering if any of that had actually just happened.

With another mystery solved I could put my feet up in theory and relax, but in true fashion another had arrived just as the first was solved.

"Come on buttercup," I said as I got into the car. "Let's head home."

CHAPTER 18

The next morning Deacon had to wake up early for work. I rose at a more normal time a few hours later, yawning and stretching as I made my way downstairs. I had just reached the top of the stairs when a voice startled.

"Hey, wakey, wakey!" the magic mirror said in her abrasive jersey accent.

I jumped out of my skin and sighed upon realizing it was the mirror. "Is the shouting really necessary at this hour?"

"Ah, quit your complaining. I think it's pretty obvious which one of us is the fun Chelsea," my magical reflection said, crossing her arms and rolling her eyes.

"I think we've established who the loud one is too. Now if you don't mind, I'm going to get some breakfast—"

"Did you think I was saying good morning just for the fun of it? I've got something for you, you dummy. Wake up already!" The magical reflection cupped her hands over her mouth, shouting the last part.

"For the love of pancakes, please stop shouting," I pleaded. "What did you find?"

The magic reflection grinned and stepped closer to her side of the mirror. "You remember how I said there's another magic mirror somewhere on the island?"

"Yeah," I recollected. "You said there are three in total. This one, Belladonna's, and then another...somewhere."

"Right! Wow, I'm amazed. I didn't think you actually listen to me."

"Most of the time it pays not to, but I guess you're useful every now and then. So, you've found this third magical mirror?"

"Uh... not quite," my reflection said, her smile faltering a little. "But I did manage to get a glimpse through it."

"What does that mean?" I asked.

"It's a little difficult to explain, but imagine you want to see inside a house, but it's locked. Maybe you walk around and find a curtain or blind that's not been closed quite properly... well I've done the magical mirror equivalent of peeping through a blind, and it let me glimpse what's directly on the other side of this mirror. I can show you, if you like."

I blinked, wiped sleep from eye and shrugged at the suggestion. If I was being honest with myself, I was still waking up. "Um, sure, whatever. What's the harm?"

"That's the spirit!" the magic mirror said excitedly. "Alright, hold onto your socks. This is what I saw!"

The reflection of my landing dimmed, and the mirror grew dark. Then another image faded into view, it showed a large round room that looked to be built out of stone. There were suits of armor, red velvet carpet, chandeliers and portraits hanging upon the walls.

"Looks fancy," I murmured. The image bubbled away, and the reflection of my landing came back into view. "Uh, so is that it?"

"What do you mean, is that it?!" my magic reflection said in exasperation. "I thought you'd be happy with this; do you know how hard I had to work to get it!"

"Thankyou?" I said, not really sure what my magic reflection wanted from me.

"That's a start!" Mirror Chelsea barked. "I think it's about time I started getting a little respect around here."

"Look I'm grateful that you went to effort to get this, but if I'm being honest the owner of the third magical mirror is kind of an inconsequential mystery in my life at the moment. It doesn't really matter, does it? I mean, I've got bigger fish to fry this week."

My enchanted reflection crossed her arms and stuck out her tongue. "Fine, that's the last time I help you, baby doll! Don't come crying to me next time you need help with something!"

"Yeah, yeah, whatever," I mumbled to myself, turning away from my childish reflection and heading downstairs. I found Artemis in the kitchen, reading a newspaper while he ate breakfast. The newspaper, titled 'Witchy Times', was floating in the air in front of him.

"The beast awakens!" Artemis announced dramatically as I made my way over to the kitchen.

"Very funny," I remarked. "How are you this fine morning?"

"Just splendid," Artemis said, finishing the last of his food and hopping over to the table to talk to me. "What's going on with you and that crazy girl in the mirror? I heard you arguing from down here."

"We weren't arguing, she just has quite an abrasive voice—she was actually quite helpful, I guess I came across as ungrateful," I said. In all fairness I *had* asked the magic mirror to try and find the other mirror for me, she'd only acted on that request.

"But you have other things on your mind, like this business with this Mordoc fellow. You need to get into this castle."

"Yes, and fast. It's the full moon tonight and he'll become even stronger, so we have to get in before then."

"Any ideas so far?" Artemis asked.

"We might have a way in now," I said. "Lizzy introduced me to one of her friends, this guy called Tony—he's really good at illusion, and we can disguise ourselves without Mordoc knowing it's magic."

"Spreadsheet Tony?"

"You know him?" I asked.

"Of course, I know Spreadsheet Tony, the guy is just about the most powerful wizard in the world, he's something else!" Artemis said loudly.

"So, you agree then?" I asked. "I thought he was very impressive too, but Tony and Lizzy downplayed his abilities a lot."

"Let me clue you in on a little secret Chelsea, witches and wizards are stuck in the past, they tend to look down on illusion and view it as a lesser form of magic—and that's because it is."

"But the things he can do, it's amazing!"

"It is amazing, but none of it is real. If I asked you to blow a hole in this wall right now you could, and the hole would be real. Well Spreadsheet Tony could explode this entire house with one snap of his fingers, and you'd be convinced it was real, but not a single brick would be out of place."

"So, what, his specialty is obviously illusion magic, what does it matter if he can't actually do any of those spells for real?" I asked.

"Hey, I agree with you one hundred percent," Artemis said. "I'm just trying to explain why the rest of the witching world looks down upon illusion. I suppose they're set in their ways."

"Well, I think he's amazing," I said, eager to rush to Tony's defense. "And I think he will play an important role in getting us inside this castle. He's going to make us look like some of Mordoc's magical mutants."

"Band name," Artemis said quickly.

"What?" I asked in confusion.

"Mordoc's Magical Mutants… that would be a killer band name. I can picture it now. Did I ever tell you I used to be in a band? Before I was a cat, I played the Glangozil, it's this thirteen-stringed instrument that looks like a gourd, but it also has a mouthpiece for—"

"I'm going to stop you right there," I said. "The day is already growing old, and I've got to somehow put together a battle plan to stop a mad wizard before sundown."

"Noted," Artemis said. "I'll save the Glangozil story for later then."

"Or, you know, just throw it into your mental garbage can and move on," I said. "I can already tell that story is going to be a long one."

"Of course, it's going to be a long one, Lardy Bard played three summers together, and they were three excellent summers!" he said boldly. "That band was the happiest time of my life!"

"I'm going to go now," I said. "I've got actual important business to take care of."

"You never make time for me!" Artemis shouted as I headed out of the kitchen.

"Yes, deliberately!" I shouted back.

* * *

I LEFT the house with no particular destination in mind. I stared up my little yellow buttercup and drove the spluttering rust bucket in the direction of town. It was a cold morning, and the heaters in the car were barely heating up the inside.

"Sorry to break it to you, Buttercup, but you're probably going to be a cube of rust before the end of this year." The car's engine gave back a timely whine, it was just the gears slipping against the old clutch, but I imagined the car was talking back to me.

But you can't cube me, I'm your beloved Buttercup!

"I know, Buttercup, and we've had some good adventures together, but I've got a little one on the way and I'm going to need something a little safer once I'm driving around with a baby. I mean no offense, but I think if you hit a matchstick, you'd completely crumple." I never exactly wanted to be one of those soccer mom types driving a huge suburban tank, but I'd been doing my research and statistically it did seem like they were the safest things to drive on the road.

Buttercup on the other hand, as much as I loved her, was a rusting death-trap and I probably shouldn't have ever set foot in her in the first place. I'd looked up the safety rating of this old car the other night and after watching a few crash test videos online my mind had already pretty much been made up.

"Do you always talk to yourself in the car?" a voice came from the back. I shrieked as Artemis jumped into the front passenger seat and blinked at me. I probably should have been used to his intrusions by now, but they always took me by surprise somehow.

"For the love of peanut butter!" I exclaimed. "Can people please stop startling me this morning! Why are you in the car?"

"I knew you were heading out, so I decided to sneak in the back so I could come along for the ride. Do I have to remind you that I was trapped in the house for like a century? You're the one that decided to free me, this is technically *your* fault."

I mean, he had a point. "Yes, and I bear the brunt of it every day. I suppose I'd be keen to get out too if I'd been trapped in for a century."

"Yeah, I knew you'd be on my side!" Artemis piped. "So where are we heading?"

"I actually haven't got any plans, I'm just letting the universe guide me this morning," I said as I turned onto the main road that ran through town. Before sunset today I had to come up with a way of stopping Mordoc, and so far, I had about ten percent of an actual plan. Without thinking I pulled over on the side of the road and stopped the engine. We were in the center of town now. There were a few blocks at the middle of town that had the most shops and attracted the most footfall, looking out the window of the car I saw the bank.

"The bank, ugh!" Artemis said and rolled his eyes. "Why are we at the bank! I can't think of a worse adventure!"

"I don't know if you recall, but I was handed a rather handsome check yesterday for helping out Dec King, so I'm going to go and cash it. Then I'll figure out what I'm doing with the rest of the day. You can stay here, and I whole heartedly encourage you to do so."

Ten minutes later I was back in the car, Artemis had fallen asleep and jumped awake as I closed the door. "Did you cash the check?" he asked.

"Yup," I said and started the car. I pulled back onto the road, again, driving without any destination in mind.

"Yee haw, we're rich cowboy!" Artemis hollered.

"*We* are not rich," I scoffed. "I mean, that check is pretty hefty, but if you consider that I'm going to have to take some time off when the baby comes then I pretty much just cashed my maternity pay. I'm thinking of upgrading the car to something a little safer too, so I'll have to budget for that. And point the third, it's my money, not yours."

"Eh, everyone knows I'm a kept cat," Artemis said with a shrug. "You make the dough, and I eat the cat food and tell funny jokes."

"When are these funny jokes coming along then?" I asked. "Right now, I feel like I'm not getting a fair deal."

"How dare you!" Artemis said in mock offense.

I don't know where the universe was taking me now, but I found myself pulling over a few minutes later in the lot of 'John Vance's' car dealership. "Wait, you're turning in Buttercup today?!" Artemis asked in surprise.

"I don't know, my intuition just sort of brought me here. I guess it wouldn't hurt to take a look, I mean I can shop around and see if there's anything I—" I stopped halfway through my sentence as I lay eyes upon the yellowest SUV I'd ever seen in my life. "Crepes on a cracker, I think I'm in love," I said, turning off the engine and climbing out of Buttercup, walking over to the giant yellow suburban tank.

"Beauty ain't she?" a car salesman said as he came across the lot. "Now if it's horsepower you're interested in this baby's got it, we're talking—"

"Let me stop you right there," I said. "I will buy this car right now. How much?"

"She's thirty-thousand dollars," the salesman said. "Cash or credit? I can do you a little discount if you take the credit."

"Isn't it usually the other way around?" I asked.

"Nah," he said. "Not these days, we getter better commission on the finance deals."

"Ah well, sorry to rain on your parade, but I'm paying cash."

"Rain on my parade? Are you kidding me? This might be the easiest sale I've ever made. I'm gonna head into that office and do a backflip once I go and get the paperwork."

I laughed. "Well, here's one condition of sale, I want to see that backflip happen. Oh, I've got a trade in too. The little yellow car just over there." I yanked my thumb in the direction of Buttercup, not taking my eyes off my new car. "Can I drive her away today?"

"Of course, you can," the salesman said, his mouth practically running with saliva at how easy this sale was for him. "That's your old car over there?"

"Yeah," I said. "I know she's not much. How much could I get for a trade in?"

The salesman stared at Buttercup for a moment, a look of marked disgust on his face. "I'll give you $100 to get that thing off my forecourt right now, put it that way," he said with a laugh. "She's making the other cars look bad."

"I would have thought she made them look better by comparison."

The salesman grimaced. "Some cars are so ugly they just happen to drag everything else down with them. No offense of course. I can offer you $150 if we strike a deal now, even though the car is pretty old it looks like you've looked after her."

"Then you've got yourself a deal, mister," I said, still not taking my eyes off Buttercup 2.0. One hour and some mind-numbing paperwork later I came out of the dealership driving my new car. Artemis hopped into Buttercup 2.0 with me and looked around at the spacious interior.

"I'm not sure about this," he said. "I miss the old Buttercup."

"Really?" I asked. "Did you know there's climate control in this car? And heated seats?" I adjusted a dial on the dashboard, heating the seat immediately underneath Artemis. His eyes widened in delight, and he started purring.

"Did I say I miss the old car? Forget about that hunk of junk. Onward to the next destination! By the way is there a dial that pours out cream?"

"I'll have to look through the manual, but I'm almost certain that's a no."

"Ah shucks," Artemis said and curled up, ready to fall asleep on his heated seat. "Just when I thought we'd found the perfect car."

We rolled off the forecourt and I started driving down the road, once again with no particular destination in mind. It was then that I realized we were only around the corner from a coffee shop where I had met Count Vassago a few weeks ago. I decided to stop by and pay him a visit. Maybe he might be able to tell me something that could get me into his castle.

A minute later I had pulled up once again after taking Buttercup

2.0 for a successful maiden voyage. I climbed out of the car and walked up to the front door of Vassago's coffee shop, knocking on the glass door three times. It was dark inside and the sign on the door was flipped to 'closed'. A few moments later I saw movement at the back of the shop and saw Jack Valentine walk up to the door. He was wearing a trench coat, a large-brimmed hat and shades. Jack unlocked the door and ushered me inside quickly, locking the door behind me as I stepped inside.

"I was starting to think you weren't going to come!" he said, his pale face stricken with panic.

"What are you talking about? I turned up here on a whim. I just got a new car actually; do you want to see it?"

"I've been trying to call you all morning," Jack said. "I sent you a dozen messages."

"Huh?" Pulling out my phone I noticed it had nudged to silent by accident. Sure enough there was a dozen missed calls from Jack, and as many messages too. "Well, what's going on?" I asked.

"It's Count Vassago," Jack said gravely. "He's dying, he's on his deathbed. I don't think he has long left. You need to come quickly."

I nodded and swallowed my dry throat. "Lead the way," I said.

CHAPTER 19

I'd only been to Vassago's coffee shop twice, and on my previous visits I'd only stayed in the main room of the shop. I followed Jack through a door on the wall behind the counter, descending down a set of stairs that seemed to go on forever, winding down and down, deeper into the unknown.

"How far down do these stairs go exactly?" I asked Jack, finding myself surprised by their depth.

"Quite a way," he said. "Don't worry, we're nearly there."

We turned down another six flights—I guess I was counting now just out of curiosity—and walked through a small stone archway. The archway opened into a large and dim underground room that had been carved out of the rock itself, the room was about fifteen feet square, and on the wall opposite from the door I saw Vassago lying in a large four poster bed. Old jazz music was playing from a record player on a table next to the bed. There were various other items of furniture around the room, and tapestries hanging from the wall. It looked like this was Vassago's make-shift home while he was waiting for his castle.

"So, you came," the old vampire said, his voice rasping more than usual. "Come and sit. I'd like to talk with you before I pass."

I looked at Jack for reassurance. He nodded and held his hand out, gesturing for me to take a seat in a chair that was next to the bed. As I walked away Jack left the room with a slight bow. I walked over to the chair, sat down, and looked around the strange subterranean bedroom. There were other doors leading from this room, tunnels that stretched further into this curious underground world.

"Where are we?" I asked.

"One of my old bases," Vassago said. "There are networks of tunnels deep under the island. No one knows where they came from, not even me."

"That's slightly terrifying," I admitted. "Where do they lead to?"

The old vampire shrugged. The only source of light in the dim room was a flickering candle, and its warm yellow light danced over the many crevices and wrinkles on Vassago's old face. "I don't know, I explored them in my youth, I even tried to map them, but I don't think I've even scratched the surface." He blinked, the red pupils of his eyes yellow and cloudy from cataracts.

"You didn't look like this last time we met," I said. I mean, the ancient vampire did look old last time we met, but he seemed significantly weaker this time. "What happened to you?"

"Time caught up to me," Vassago said wistfully. "It happens to every vampire eventually. Those that assume we are immortal are greatly mistaken. We have long lives, but the reaper will come for us eventually. Once the vampire reaches the end of their life the end comes on quickly. This in part is why I wanted to get back into the castle."

"You wanted to die in the castle?" I asked.

Vassago nodded, it was a very slight movement, I could tell he was conserving his strength as much as possible. "I have known for quite some time now that the end of my life is near. I would have been more forthright with you, but it's in my best interest to keep my weaknesses close to my chest, hopefully you understand this. After a lifetime of keeping secrets from enemies, I find it hard to always be completely truthful. A vampire does not want to disclose his weaknesses, you never know who might be listening."

"I suppose I understand that," I said, letting my eyes wander across the room before I looked back at him again. "Why did you lie to me about the castle?" I asked.

Vassago looked at me with curiosity. "Did I lie?"

"You said that you left the castle to go travelling, and that in your absence the Brewdock witches—your former servants—stole the castle from you. You said they were a malignant force, an evil that will threaten this island."

"And I suppose you have spoken with these Brewdock witches, and they have a different account?" he rasped.

"Yes. Belladonna Brewdock said you fled the castle because you couldn't bear the power of the demon living underneath it. She said it intimidated you, frightened you. I've been to the isle to see them, and from my impression the Brewdocks aren't a threat at all, they've been caretakers for the castle all this time, looking after it in your absence. The real threat is a mad wizard, someone that has taken over the castle recently."

Vassago lifted an intrigued brow. "Is that so? Well, I—" Vassago paused, his cloudy eyes moving around the room has he explored inner-avenues of his distant recollection. After several long minutes of silent reflection he resumed speaking. "Well in that case I apologize."

"So, you did lie?" I asked him.

"Perhaps lie is not the best word. You now know about my ailing condition, well, with that ailing condition I find my mind is beginning to degrade too. I have consulted with my physician about it, she said I am sundowning."

"You're what now?"

"Sundowning. Losing my mind, early signs of dementia. When that begins people start to forget things, fabricate false memories based around fear and paranoia. I think in my old age I have forgotten the true nature of things."

"So, you sent me on a wild goose chase," I said.

"It would seem so, but—and correct me if I am wrong—you mentioned a mad wizard has taken over the castle, it sounds like there is still a force that you have to contend with, even if it wasn't the one that I suspected in the first place. Is my logic correct there, or am I wrong? It's hard to tell these days."

I pursed my lips, before answering. "I suppose you are right. Tell me, if you're dying then why does it matter if you go back to the castle? You haven't lived there in centuries. Is it even a home to you?"

"Home is where the heart is," Vassago said, his dry voice crackling through the air like broken branches. "My one true love in life, Tatyana, she is buried in the crypts below the castle. It is my wish to go there so I can die at her side and be laid to rest next to her. *That* Miss Sponks, is the real reason I want my castle back."

So, there it was, the truth that Vassago had been keeping from me all this time. Taking back the castle wasn't part of some grand plan for domination, or a ruse to get revenge on the Brewdock witches. When I stripped everything back the very nature of things was quite simple. Vassago was an old man, and a dying one at that, all he wanted was to die next to his loved one.

"I actually came here to ask you for help," I said. "I don't know how to get into the castle. The wizard that has holed himself inside is cunning, and he's using the power of the demon to strengthen his position. My magic is no match against him. Is there any other way I can get inside?"

Vassago thought about it for a moment then shrugged. "My mind used to be a blade, Miss Sponks, a blade that was so sharp it could slice the air itself. These days the answers don't come to me so easily, it's like a curtain has been drawn over my thoughts, and I can't quite see past it. That said... I can't think of any other way you can get in there without the aid of magic. Castle Vassago is a fortress, I designed it to be impenetrable."

I let out a deflated sigh and chewed on my lip while tapping my foot on the rug positioned underneath Vassago's bed. "Well, I'm all out of ideas then. I don't know how to help you, and with the full moon tonight this mad wizard believes he will be able to raise Bahmut and take over the island."

Vassago chuckled quietly to himself, the sound breaking out into a cough. "Sounds like you're in quite the predicament, eh?" he asked. "Do me a favor, go over to that cabinet on the far wall, open the middle drawer. There is an old red book inside. Fetch it for me and bring it here."

I got out of my chair, walked across the room and retrieved the book from the drawer, taking it back to Vassago's bedside. I handed him the book and he pushed himself up into more of a sitting position. He opened the book and inside I saw what I assumed were photographs.

"Memories?" I asked him.

"Yes, I thought you might like to see pictures of Tatyana and myself when we were younger. We were quite the beautiful couple, if I don't say so myself." Vassago passed me the book and I took it.

"I thought vampires didn't show up in photographs?"

"We don't, but I had the most amazing painter, a young wizard man that served as my accomplice for over a century. That boy could capture the world in the most realistic fashion. Look at Tatyana, wasn't she beautiful?"

I flicked through the pages, admiring the realistic paintings that depicted Vassago and his former love in their youth. I had to admit that they were a startingly handsome couple, the kind that would turn the heads of everyone on the street. "These are from inside the castle?" I asked Vassago.

"Yes, the majority, that is where Tatyana and I spent most of our time together. Mordoc, he was so gifted when it came to capturing the light, but even in his best efforts he could never fully capture Tatyana's angelic beauty."

I nodded for a moment as I flicked onto another page, but then I stopped and looked up at Vassago. "Hang on a second, Mordoc?"

"Yes, that was the name of the boy that did the portraits," he recollected.

"That's the name of the mad wizard currently residing in the castle," I said.

"Impossible," Vassago said. "Mordoc died, I was there the night he passed, but—"

"But what?" I asked.

"He *did* have a son, if my recollection is correct, though even his son would be an old man now, this would have to be a… grandson?" Vassago was looking up at the ceiling as he tried his best to venture through the fog of time.

"Wouldn't Belladonna recognize the name?" I asked him. "She's seen Mordoc, she knows his name."

"Mordoc the portrait artist died long before her time," Vassago said. "She wouldn't know him."

"But why would the grandson come back to take the castle?" I asked. "It doesn't make any sense, did you and his grandfather end on bad terms?"

"No, not at all!" Vassago said, almost seeming hurt by the accusation. "I counted Mordoc amongst my best friends, although—"

"Although?"

"His mistress held me in sour contempt, she was a deeply religious woman, she did not like that her husband was in the employ of a character such as myself. I rewarded Mordoc handsomely for his talents, I made him a rich man, but his wife said it was never enough! When he passed, I never heard from her again. Surely her contempt for me couldn't have passed down the generations?"

I wasn't so sure. "If this woman hated you as much as you say, then I wouldn't put it past her. She could have brought up her child with all sorts of false ideas, and those ideas in turn could be passed down to the grandchild, this mad wizard that controls your castle now. The one thing we haven't been able to figure out is how he got inside in the first place."

Vassago's cloudy eyes flicked around in his skull, they widened as he came upon an idea. "The mirror," he said.

"The what now?" I asked.

"Mordoc, the portrait artist, he never lived at the castle, he had a home on the main island. I gifted him a magic mirror that would let him travel between his home and the castle. I still have a magic mirror in the castle, perhaps the grandson found his way through that."

"Wait a minute," I said. "You have a magic mirror in the castle?"

"Yes! It is the only way a vampire can see their reflection. Only Mordoc and I knew about it, I kept it in my bedroom, a secret even from the Brewdock witches," he said.

Flicking through the portrait book I came across a familiar background all of a sudden. I saw a round stone room dressed with portraits and tapestries. "Hold the phone, is this your bedroom?" I asked.

"No," Vassago said as he looked at the picture. "That is the study, why?"

"My own magic mirror showed me an image this morning, and it looked just like this study. I think this Mordoc Junior might have moved the mirror into there. Crepes on a cracker, she was useful!"

"What?" Vassago said in confusion.

"Never mind, what's the passphrase to your mirror?"

"Speculo," Vassago answered. "That will let you through."

I stood up quickly from the chair, putting the book on the table next to Vassago's bed. "I have to go; I think I know how to deal with Mordoc now."

"You can get into the castle with the magic mirror!" he said.

"I can, but I think he will fully be anticipating that. I've got another idea instead. I already have another way into the castle, but I didn't have a way to deal with Mordoc until now. Now I think I know how I can defeat him. Hold on a little longer Vassago, I will have your castle back soon."

Without another word I ran out of the room and began the long ascent up the underground staircase, back to the surface and the world above. I finally had a way to defeat Mordoc, I just had to hope my plan would go off without a hitch.

CHAPTER 20

"First of all, thank you all for gathering here. It means a lot to me," I said to the group standing in my kitchen.

"I'm literally here all the time," Lizzy said.

"Yeah," Glenda added. "Same."

"I feel like I end up popping in here at least once a week," Chad Chaplin said.

"Well, it's new for me!" Spreadsheet Tony said gleefully.

"Thank you, Tony," I said. "The rest of you can be quiet, stop ruining my moment. I'm trying to do a pep talk here."

"Why can't I be involved in this again?" Artemis asked.

"Because you're a walking liability," Deacon said from the table.

"Hey, at least I've seen this castle up close. You didn't get invited!"

"I was away, and I don't have a lick of magic. What am I going to do, shoot the evil wizard to death?" Deacon joked.

Everyone suddenly looked at me as if that was an option I hadn't yet considered. "I'm pretty sure we couldn't just shoot him to death," I said, laughing nervously. I looked at Lizzy and Glenda for backup. "Right?"

"Ethics aside for a moment, this little weasel seems cunning enough to have protection spells around him, bullets won't do much," Glenda said.

"Just to be clear we're not going to shoot this guy dead. In the best-case scenario, no one gets hurt. Just because we have a criminally insane wizard on our hands doesn't mean we have free reign to start dishing out pain," I said.

"But do we have a codeword set up or anything, in case you change your mind?" Glenda asked.

"Look we're reasonable people, and we're accomplished magic users. We can take care of Mordoc without resorting to his tactics. After we get in there it's a simple case of restraining him with magic and putting an end to this nonsense once and for all," I clarified.

"And what if he resists restraint?" Lizzy asked.

"Well then we get creative. But we're not shooting anyone, and we're not going in there deliberately looking to cause pain," I said.

"Hot sauce," Glenda said. I turned my head and stared at her.

"What is that supposed to mean?"

"Hot sauce, that's the codeword I just came up with. Once you change your mind about lethal force, you just say the codeword 'Hot sauce' and we're all on the same page," Glenda said.

"We're not using lethal force," I said.

"Well not *lethal*, but you know, pulling out the big guns. You've seen those bounty hunter shows, those guys and gals do whatever it takes to bring down the purp!" Glenda punched her fist into her open hand.

I stared at my aunt for a moment, wondering why this was the team I'd assembled. If I was being honest with myself this was the best I had, and that wasn't a bad thing. Lizzy and Glenda were accomplished witches, and I knew they'd have my back. Chad was valuable too, and Spreadsheet Tony was perhaps the most valuable teammate of all, without his illusion magic this plan would be nothing.

"So, we're all clear on the plan then?" I asked the group. Since leaving Vassago's bedside I'd put together a plan in my head, arranging all the components on the drive back to the house while I called everyone I would need on the way. As soon as everyone was here, I'd gone over the plan three of four times, just to make sure we all knew what was going on.

"I mean it's pretty straightforward, what's not to get?" Chad asked. "My problem is that *your* part of the plan is incredibly dangerous. Like, we're talking top-tier magic that is super risky. Are you sure you're comfortable with that?"

Lizzy put her hand up. "I can't believe I'm saying this, but I actually agree with Chad—the spell that you have proposed Chelsea is dangerous." Lizzy was looking down at the open spell book on the table in front of her, the book opened to the magical maneuver I wanted to use. "I mean, it all looks simple enough, but there are risks associated with this."

"You're all a bunch of pansies," Glenda said dismissively. "If Chelsea thinks she can do it then she can do it. What's the problem?"

"You're hardly a reliable point of view," Artemis said to Glenda. "I've met boxes of frogs that are saner than you."

"What's that supposed to mean?!" Glenda said. "I'm perfectly sane!"

"Uh, I've seen your record," Chad said from the edge of the room. "How you are not in prison astounds me."

Glenda winked at Chad and blew him a kiss. "Darling when you can sweet talk like me you can get yourself out of anything. Those high judges at the MCI love me!"

"Let's bring this back on track," I said to the group. "I know what I'm getting myself in for, and it's fine—as long as we all stick to the plan everything will go off without a hitch. I want everyone to take a glibstone, they'll help me stay in touch with you." I opened the string bag I had in my hand and pulled out five of the little yellow stones. Each was big enough to comfortably fit inside the ear and would allow us to communicate with one another magically should we need to— (Artemis had found them in Griselda's safe, proving himself useful for once).

"Is that everything?" Glenda asked.

I nodded my head. "Now is as good as time as any. Everyone follow me upstairs and we'll head through the mirror to Belladonna's hut. I'll have to fly over of course, but it won't take me more than a few minutes to get there.

Upstairs I activated the magic mirror, opening a doorway to Belladonna's hut on Vassago Isle. One by one everyone disappeared through the mirror frame until it was just me and the magical reflection.

"I don't know what's going to happen when you do this," my magic reflection said in her stark jersey accent. "You know it's a risk, more than you're letting on."

"Well, we don't have much other choice," I said. "Come on, shrink down. I need to hop on a broom and fly over there to meet them." I took a step back and watched as the full-sized mirror dropped off the wall and started walking on its corners, shrinking rapidly down in size until it was no bigger than the size of a phone. I picked up the mirror and put it in my pocket.

Outside the house I kissed Deacon goodbye and held my hand out to summon a broom, one appeared a moment later. "You sure you're going to be okay?" Deacon asked.

"Everything is going to be fine, another day, another mystery. I love you."

"I love you too," he said.

With that I kicked off from the ground, soaring up towards the sky, my broom pointed in the direction of Vassago Isle out to the west and over the water.

Lookout Mordoc, I'm coming for you.

* * *

A FEW MINUTES later my broom touched down on the ground outside Belladonna's house. I made my way inside and found Glenda, Lizzy, Chad, and Spreadsheet Tony waiting for me.

"Here she comes, the woman of the hour," Glenda said as I walked through the door. "We were just practicing our illusions with Tony here."

"Great stuff," I said, pleased to hear that everyone was keeping on track. "Let's see how it's going then."

Tony waved his hands and everyone in the room seemed to change in front of my eyes. Lizzy became some sort of half-rhino woman, Glenda's bottom half became a walrus, and Chad's upper half became a pig. "Chad, I can hardly tell a difference," I joked. Tony waved his hands again and they all changed back.

"I made the same joke!" Lizzy said excitedly.

"Does everything look okay?" Tony asked. "You're sure you don't need a disguise?"

"Not with this new plan," I answered. "I already have my way in, and if everything goes to plan you guys don't even need to go inside, you're just a distraction out front." I turned and looked at Belladonna. "Are you still able to take them up to the front of the castle?"

"Yes," she said and nodded. "This plan of yours is dangerous you know, not for us—but for you."

I shrugged. "I'll be fine. It's nothing a High Witch can't handle, right? You guys set off now and I'll get ready to do my part of the plan. We can all keep in touch with the glibstones."

With that everyone left the shack and began the journey up the track to the front of the castle. Once they were out of sight, I held the tip of my forefinger against the small yellow stone nestled in my ear to test out our magical communication channel.

"Lizzy, can you hear me?"

"Yeah," her voice came back a moment later. "We're about halfway up the track now. Tony's about to start the illusion. Are you ready with the mirror?"

"I'm going to get ready now. Let me know when you're at the door."

I went into the small room at the back of the shack, where Belladonna's magic mirror was stored. As I walked in, I saw her reflection sitting on the bed through the mirror. She looked up at me. "You know there's a reason they tell you not to face two magic mirrors together. It's extremely unpredictable, there's no telling what's going to happen."

"Well, you're just my doorway into the castle. My mirror and Vassago's will do the rest, there's no risk for you."

"No," Belladonna's reflection said back. "But I'm still enabling this suicide mission of yours."

"Just get me into the castle," I said. "I'll do the rest."

"What's the password for Vassago's mirror?"

"Speculo," I said, repeating the codeword Vassago had given to me.

With a huff Belladonna's magical reflection got up from the bed, closed her eyes and held her hands out. A moment later the surface of the mirror rippled, and the image went dark. After another few seconds a new image rippled over the surface, it was the round stone room from inside Vassago's castle.

Now it didn't look like I was staring at a reflection at all, the mirror simply seemed like a doorway through which I could walk, and that's because it was.

"Chelsea we're in position," Glenda's voice came through the glib-stone in my ear. "Belladonna's just put a magical flare in the air to get this guy's attention. There's a half a dozen magical mutants on his doorstep, there's no way he won't take this bait. Oh, oh, he's coming!"

"Now," Belladonna's voice came over the stone. "Through the mirror now, he's taken the bait."

I quickly rushed through the mirror and found myself standing in the round stone room on the other side. It was much larger than I had anticipated, and taller too. As my feet hit the floor I turned around and saw Belladonna's shack was gone, I was now looking at a reflection of the round stone room. In that reflection I saw the magic reflection of Vassago.

"Just in who the devil are you?" he said. "Who do you think you are breaking into my castle like this?! Mordoc! Mordoc! Come quickly!" The mirror's frame started pulsing brightly and I cursed, I knew that Mordoc would be coming now.

"I'm trying to help you idiot, your master—your real one tasked me with getting this castle back from Mordoc."

"Well, he's coming now, you two can duke it out together!" Vassago's magic reflection said. "You should know that he's very powerful!

He's been taking power from Bahmut, too much power if you ask me, the fellow's gone insane!"

"It's fine, I know how to deal with it," I said. "In fact, you're going to help me, I'm going to have to move you."

"Move me? Move me! Where?! That brute already moved me from the bedroom into this ghastly room!"

"Get ready for the ride of your life then, because you're going five feet to the left." With my magic I lifted Vassago's magic mirror up and floated it back until it was resting against the wall. Then I took my own magic mirror out of my pocket and placed it on the floor. "Hey, unfold, hurry up. He's coming!"

The small palm-sized mirror started unfolding until it was the size of a full body mirror. "Alright, let's do this!" my reflection said in her abrasive jersey accent.

"Hey, careful there!" Vassago's reflection said. "You nearly had the two mirrors facing one another. You can't do that; do you know how dangerous that it?!"

"Yes, and that's the plan, now shut up and let me do this." With my hands I lifted my magic mirror into the air and floated it across the room until it was on the other side. Before setting it down I covered it with a cloth and then let it rest on the floor. Now both mirrors were on opposite sides of the room and facing one another. I was directly in the middle of the room, standing between them, once I removed the cloth I would be caught between both reflections.

Directly in front of me a huge stone archway opened onto a set of stairs that led down. I heard footsteps rapidly ascending and then I saw Mordoc—the real one, not a vision this time—sprint up and stop at the top of stairs. He doubled over as he caught his breath.

"A nasty trick!" he said as he straightened up and walked forward. He brushed his platinum blonde hair back and took a few steps before stopping again. There was about twenty feet between us now. "What exactly do you think you've accomplished? You're inside, sure, but I'm more powerful than you are now. A few days ago, I would have been scared, but right now I've got nothing to fear. One of you versus one of me… this is going to be a quick battle."

"I know," I said. "That's why I brought more than one of me. If you're going to play dirty, then so will I."

Mordoc's brow knit in confusion. "What are you talking about? There's only one of—you know what, it doesn't matter. I'm not going to let you stall for any more time, let's just hurry up and get this is over with." The mad wizard curled both his hands to his side of his body, and they began to grow bright with violent red light. I had no idea what spell he was about to unleash, but I could tell it wasn't a friendly one.

With my left hand I used magic to pull back the cloth covering my mirror, trapping myself between the reflections of both frames. Looking left and right I suddenly saw an infinite number of myself reflected on both sides, the repeating images stretching on into darkness. The reflected Chelsea's started coming out of both mirrors—lots of Chelsea's. Hundreds.

Mordoc didn't cast the spell in his hands, instead he just stared in utter bewilderment as more and more copies of myself entered the room from the magic mirror. With the room completely packed I stepped forward, so I was out of the reflection. As I took that step the hundred other copies of me stepped forward too.

"Right," I said, and with that word a hundred other versions of me said it too. My voice boomed around the room. "I think it's safe to say you're outnumbered. So how are we going to do this? Do you give up? Or do I kick your butt?"

The mad wizard's eyes grew wild, and his eyes began to glow again. "You won't take this from me, you won't! It's mine! Mine!" He thrust his hands out and a deadly ball of magical red light exploded forwards. I didn't even have to react, because my hundred clones dealt with the attack for me, using their magic to deflect the assault.

"Get him," I said to them, and at once my hundred copies all cast a hundred binding spells to capture the mad wizard. Mordoc roared out in fury, the power of one hundred witches far too much even for his demon-imbued strength. As soon as he hit the ground I turned my attention on the most dangerous thing in the room—the copies of me.

"Alright, time to go back," I said to the reflections. Without so much as a response they all started filing back through the mirror until it was just me and Mordoc left standing in the room.

I had stopped the mad wizard; I had got back the castle. The island was safe once more, and I could finally rest.

It was just another day on Pendle Island.

CHAPTER 21

"I have to give it to her, the podcast episode is pretty great," Artemis said from the living room floor. Deacon, Lizzy, Artemis, and I were all listening to Adina's episode covering the Dec King mystery, at is had just been released today. I had to admit Adina had put together an entertaining show.

"So now you're a super famous world-wide detective I bet the cases will be really pouring in. How you're going to schedule that around a child I don't know!" Lizzy remarked.

"Hey, once this kid comes along, I'll be taking some well-earned time off," I said. "I can't run around chasing killers once I'm in the third trimester."

"Yeah, she'll just make me do that part when she can't run," Deacon joked.

"I am capable of taking time off!" I said in my defense. "Y'all treat me like I'm some sort of workaholic."

"I mean you've been refreshing your website inbox every five minutes waiting for a new case," Lizzy joked. "You've been itching for another mystery ever since you solved the whole Dec King thing."

"Yeah," Artemis joined in. "And now you've sorted out the problem with Vassago's castle you're really bored! There's literally nothing for you to do."

"I'm fine," I insisted. "I can always go out and buy a ten-thousand-piece puzzle or something. Or I can read a mystery book."

"Haven't you already been through everyone in the library?" Deacon chuckled. "And you never finish them either, you always stop reading halfway through."

"Because I figure it out! It's no fun once I figure it out!" I said.

Lizzy suddenly jumped up from the couch and looked at Artemis. "Artemis! Look at the time, it's nearly five! We've got that thing!"

Artemis also jumped to his feet. "Oh yeah!" He looked at Deacon and me before scrambling out of the room with Lizzy. "Got to go!"

"…What was that all about?" Deacon asked after they had left.

"I don't know. They're probably up to something weird," I said. "The less I know the better. Wait, did they just leave through the front door? What in the…" A moment later the front doorbell rang. Deacon got up to answer it and then came back to the living room.

"It's… it's our wedding planner," he said. "She wants us both out the front."

"What?" I said, wheezing as Deacon helped me out of the deep sofa. We both walked to the front door and sure enough there was Gloria, our wedding planner. "Gloria! I wasn't expecting to hear from you for some time! How is our surprise wedding going? Got a date for us yet?"

"I'll have to admit you've both had me stumped," Gloria said, fanning a hand through her flawless blonde hair. Gloria was wearing a cobalt-blue pant suit, and she looked like a million dollars. "I thought let's go big, a huge church wedding, but then it didn't feel right. Then I thought you're the kind of kids that want a low-budget wedding, something in a bowling alley, something funky like that."

I grimaced at both those ideas. "No, I want something—"

"Completely unexpected," Gloria said, finishing the end of my sentence. "Something totally out of the blue!"

"Yes!" I said excitedly. "But—"

"But surrounded by friends and family as well, so *they* all have to be in on it."

"Sounds great!" Deacon said. "So, what did you have in mind?"

"Your bags are already packed, and your closest friends and family are already on their way," Gloria explained.

"To…where?" I asked.

"Hawaii!" Gloria said with a theatrical flourish, she produced two plane tickets and handed one to each of us. "Come with me, your plane leaves in the hour. Your wedding is in two days' time!"

"Wait…" I said, shock suddenly coming over me in waves. "This is really happening?" I looked at Deacon, who seemed equally taken aback, though in a positive way.

"It most certainly is!" Gloria said. "Now hurry up and get in the car. We haven't got all day!"

Maybe this should have been expected for hiring a less-than-conventional wedding planner in the first place, but I had to admit that part of me loved this mystery and romance of this impromptu holiday.

Hawaii, here we come!

CLICK HERE to read the penultimate Book 11: Where There's a Witch, There's a Way.

THANKS FOR READING

Thanks for reading, I hope you enjoyed the book.

It would really help me out if you could leave an honest review with your thoughts and rating on Amazon.

Every bit of feedback helps!

ALSO BY MARA WEBB

~ Ongoing ~

Hallow Haven Witch Mysteries

Wicked Witches of Pendle Island

An English Enchantment

Compass Cove Cozy Mysteries

~ Completed ~

Wicked Witches of Pendle Island

Wildes Witches Mysteries

Raven Bay Mysteries

Wicked Witches of Vanish Valley

MAILING LIST

Want to be notified when I release my latest book? Join my mailing list. It's for new releases only. No spam:

https://landing.mailerlite.com/webforms/landing/w3x8g9

I'll also send you a free 120,000 word book as a thank you for signing up.

marawebbauthor.com

amazon.com/-/e/B081X754NL
facebook.com/marawebbauthor
twitter.com/marawebbauthor
bookbub.com/authors/mara-webb